Ghost Train

By Keelan Berry

Enjoy the ride! 🙂

Keelan

Copyright © 2017 by Keelan Berry

The purchaser of this book is subject to the condition that he/she shall in no way resell it, nor any part of it, nor make copies of it to distribute freely.

This book is a work of fiction. Any similarity between the characters and settings within its pages and places or persons, living or dead, is unintentional and coincidental.

I would like to thank my 'backroom staff' again, because without them this wouldn't be possible:

My Editor and Dad, Mike; who once again found the time to read and edit the book for me.

My Illustrator and Dad's Fiancé, Jenny; who made yet another amazing front cover.

My 'Legal Guy', 'IT Guy', Co-Editor and Boyfriend, Matt, who, with his law knowledge was able to help me with much of the book's content, and helped again with the poems at the start of each part, as well as helping me deal with IT issues when it comes to publishing the book.

My 'Expert' and Friend, Connor, whose advice I sought on much of the crime part of the book, thanks to his career as a police sergeant (one day, we hope, anyway!)

Last but not least, My Associates, who didn't actually do anything but just wanted a special mention: my Mom, Kelly (who is terrified of clowns, and therefore inspired much of the novel), and Brother, Vaughan (who has been a big help in pointing out – and mocking – many errors in my other books so I can correct them!)

Author's Note

'Ghost Train' is a horror/crime novel, fictional as always. I have taken some inspiration from the real-life 'killer clown craze' in October, 2016 as well as 'slasher' films again (as I did in my book 'Slasher') and many crime shows I watch on TV. It is set in the fictional county of Southumberland, fictional town of Trexham and, primarily, the fictional city of Tornwich.

Contents

Prologue _____ 1

PART ONE _____ 9

Chapter One _____ 10

Chapter Two _____ 27

Chapter Three _____ 52

Chapter Four _____ 88

Chapter Five _____ 119

Tornwich – The Interlude _____ 124

PART TWO _____ 143

Chapter Six _____ 144

Chapter Seven _____ 159

Chapter Eight _____ 171

Chapter Nine _____ 185

Chapter Ten _____ 194

Epilogue _____ 206

Ghost Train

"There is no terror in the bang, only in the anticipation of it."

Alfred Hitchcock

Prologue

Could he still hear her?

She could hear herself, although she didn't want to; the heavy, fast breathing, the high-pitched squeaks occasionally squeezing through her tight throat, the blood squelching in her knotted hair as she raised her head.

She saw the gap in the tent. It was unzipped.

She wanted to run, but so many things could go wrong.

What if he was out there?

How far could she even get?

She didn't yet know the full extent of her injuries – worse yet she didn't even know where she was.

Well, Trexham, she knew that much. But she'd never been here before, she'd only come here with her friends because it was the first night of the 'Southumberland-Wald Forest Halloween Tour' and they'd wanted to go.

She had been surprised to find that the fairground-like tour was starting off in such a small town, but understood why upon arrival. Everyone, including her group of friends from college, were talking about 'The Bunny-Man' and a bridge in the small town that he supposedly haunted.

According to the local urban legend, 'The Bunny-Man' was an insane man who had been imprisoned for murdering his family one Easter. Afterwards, he had escaped from a crashed train transporting mental patients across the bridge. The man took Wald Forest, which the bridge runs through, as his new home. Ever since then, it has been rumoured he makes a return on the night of every Halloween to stalk the bridge and terrorise the locals with an axe, hence the tour starting there. Despite it still being almost two weeks until Halloween night, she guessed that the tour and the locals were playing it safe against the urban legend, being superstitious and not wanting to tempt fate and summon the demonic entity of 'The Bunny-Man' by holding the event in Trexham on the night synonymous with the costumed killer. On the other hand, she had supposed there was the business-minded aspect of starting the tour in such a location; it would create much hype and draw a lot of attention towards the event across the month of October whilst it toured Trexham and Tornwich – the two parts of Southumberland that were actually a part of the forest.

These were things she had been able to consider earlier in the night, away from the terror she had experienced since then.

Slowly, she pushed herself up and backwards so that she could lean her head on the back of the tent and keep her eye on the open gap at the other end.

She listened closely, and could hear nothing but the wind.

Sick bastard is probably waiting for me to run just so he can capture me again, she thought.

But it was as though the darkness she could see through the slit was taunting her, calling out to her.

She knew she was in a woodland area – she had seen the trees when he had entered and exited the tent, pulling the flaps wide enough so she could see that there was more than just darkness beyond the menacing silhouetted mass of her captor.

She was in Wald Forest.

If she was going to make an attempt at escape, she knew she would have to just run and not stop.

Could she pull it off?

Maybe he's gone back to the tour.

She thought that would be too good to be true, but there was a chance…

The night had started off so well, arriving in Trexham with her friends and going to a local pub some of them had heard of: 'The Bunny's Head', obviously inspired by the urban legend that the small town was so well-known for. It was in there that the enthusiastic bartender (who, she later discovered, was the relatively new owner of the pub, having only taken over the pub over the summer following the mysterious disappearance of his predecessor, or so he claimed anyway!) was telling hordes of customers about how, in the weeks after his escape supposedly many decades ago, the killer would leave half-eaten bunny rabbits strung from the trees of Wald Forest, warning off anyone who dared to trespass on his land. That short, horrific and surely apocryphal tale explained the sign hanging outside the door of the pub: a chopped-off bunny's head lying in a pool of blood on a field of bright green grass. *Charming!*

"Is there any proof of all this?" One sceptical sounding customer had asked – a middle-aged Father who didn't appear to be too thrilled about having to bring his family to such an event.

The barman had appraised the man for a few moments, before smiling knowingly and turning around, unpinning a thin piece of paper from a small board and placing it carefully, so as to avoid any spilt beer, on the bar so that everyone could see.

The newspaper front page was dated 1989 – a quarter of a century ago – but the significance of the article was the headline: 'Bunny-Man Returns!'

"Some Halloweens," The man began, "A figure is seen. Always Halloween night. Always the same description. Always the same story. This era," He tapped the date of the newspaper cut-out, "Was the worst. The '70s, '80s – so many people claimed to have seen him. *It*. Someone in a giant bunny costume, most times wielding an axe, as though warning people off. Scaring them away from the bridge – his home."

The pub fell silent at that point. Not quiet. *Silent*. Even the sceptic who had started the discussion seemed drawn into the story, a little uncomfortable with what he had been told.

The barman laughed to break the silence, pinned the clipping back to the board, and told them that dozens of articles could be found online about reported 'sightings' and 'incidents' involving the 'Bunny-Man'. Clearly pleased that his words had had the desired effect he continued to chuckle to himself as he moved along the bar collecting empty glasses.

She didn't know what she'd been expecting, but the pub had not been as grand as she thought that it would be. It was small and hardly any different to the local pubs back home (apart from the severed head of a rabbit being used to advertise it). However, she'd still enjoyed her time in there; the atmosphere was friendly and everyone talked to one another, speaking of the local urban legend as well as discussing the different parts of the country they had all come from.

Then, when seven o'clock drew near and the sky had grown dark, they all began to flock out of the pub and make their way to Southumberland Zoo. There were many fields in and around the zoo, which was surrounded by Wald Forest, being used to host the opening night of the event. Originally, she had thought it was strange that an event was being hosted so close to many different animals at night. However, after reading the attraction's website it became clear just how enormous the zoo and Wald Forest were and that the attraction itself was situated quite deep into the zoo, bordering on and with some parts of the event going slightly inside the forest; so they wouldn't come into contact with any of the animals.

Most people seemed to have bought their tickets online and so exchanged them for wristbands upon arriving at the booths, surprisingly few others, who had presumably turned up more on a whim, purchased their wristbands at the gate. The direction of the entrance booths had been marked by signs near the zoo and on some of the trees as they walked along the road, and the booths themselves were set up slightly beyond the tree line of Wald Forest, so that they looked dark and eerie, but not deep enough so that were not easily visible. Upon entering the vast woodland there were a number of staff dressed up in Halloween and horror themed costumes to guide them around the side of the zoo (presumably to keep them away from the animals - or maybe to keep the animals away from them, she remembered thinking ghoulishly!) and to the fields where the attraction had been set up.

Most of the staff had stumped for the obvious Halloween costumes that you'd expect to see anywhere at this time of year, such as vampires and zombies, though she knew worse was to come at the event; the website had described that there would be an ordinary fairground at the event, accompanied by three horror-themed 'maze' events. The website had been vague about these, but leaflets handed out with the wristbands at the booths provided more detail: 'The Bunny-Man Bridge', perhaps predictably, was one of these 'mazes', although she doubted it would feature the actual bridge – as she'd already thought that night, the locals and the tour were trying to scare people, but not risk calling an infamous, costumed maniac from his sanctuary.

It was inside one of these mazes that she, and some of her friends, had been taken.

Forcefully grabbed, silenced and dragged outside and through the trees of Wald Forest before being knocked out or tied and gagged and thrown into tents.

For better or for worse, she wasn't quite sure which, she had been put in a tent by herself. But her friends could still be near, placed in any one of the other tents – there were three or four, she hadn't been able to see properly.

She was fairly certain there was more than the one attacker, and she had definitely heard some of her friends. Thinking back, however, she wasn't entirely sure that there was another assailant, even though she couldn't figure out how only one man would be able to take more than one of them. She was uncertain as to how many of the group he'd actually taken; three, maybe four or more by the sounds of the voices and the quick glimpses of others she had seen, but again she couldn't be sure. It had all happened so fast, and her eyes and ears hadn't been able to focus properly on anything, everything was a blur. Worse yet again, she didn't know how far she and her friends had been dragged through the trees, although it felt as though she'd struggled against the man holding her for an immense amount of time with no success.

If there was more than one attacker, she hadn't seen them.

She'd just seen *him*.

The thought of him sent shivers down her spine.

He's out there.

Just run!!!

But what if he caught her again?

Was there more pain and torture he could inflict upon her?

He's done his worst, she thought, *all he's got left is killing me.*

Slowly and shakily, she stood.

Her heart thudded heavily.

This is it.

She didn't feel steady on her legs, but they'd enabled her to stand, and she felt sure they would carry her far enough into the trees so she could then use them to hide in the darkness from her captor.

Should she search the other tents for her friends?

She thought she'd heard them, as well as her, screaming at some point that night while she lay helpless in the tent; but nothing from that night had been clear.

What if he was torturing them as he had tortured her right now?

She hadn't been awake while he'd done the worst to her, but she knew it had happened from the state her clothes were in when she woke up. But even if her clothes had seemed untouched, she would have still been able to tell, she could *feel* it.

Had he taken any of the other girls? She hoped not.

With a great effort she pushed all thoughts from her mind and mustered every last ounce of strength and resolve that she could, mentally pleading with her legs to propel her from this hell. She leapt forward, arms outstretched.

In one hope-filled moment, the tent flaps flung open, exposing the light of the moon.

Her feet landed on the floor.

I'm free!

Then, maniacal, high-pitched laughter.

Then, a white face running towards her.

Then, an axe, to the head.

Then, nothing.

PART ONE

'The police are in panic,

The public can't relax,

For down in the forest,

Someone wields an axe.'

Chapter One

"Deputy,"

Deputy Chief Constable Ralph Cox of the Southumberland Constabulary looked up, "Come in, Sergeant." He was sat at his desk, black uniform jacket hanging from the back of his chair and cap resting next to the papers he was looking over on the desk.

Detective Sergeant James Jackson entered the office and sat down opposite Cox; his large, black beard in stark contrast to Cox's pale, white face, and his shaved head shining in comparison to Cox's thin, receding, slicked-back grey hair, "Sir, the axe murders…".

"Stop, Jackson." Cox had a deep, strong voice for a man who looked as old as he did. He waved a hand, dismissing Jackson's claim before he even had a chance to make it. Cox leaned forward across the desk, and clasped his long, bony-fingered, wrinkled hands across one another and pierced Jackson with his ice-cold blue gaze, "I've told you before not to come to me about your cases, you go to Detective Inspector Hughes, he's in charge of the axe-murder case."

Cox released his hands from their locked grip and shuffled through some of his papers, apparently as a further sign of dismissal towards Jackson.

"I keep doing that, sir." Jackson stood slightly and shuffled around in his back pockets as Cox let out a sigh of disappointment and threw his papers back down on the desk, reclining in his chair, "But he keeps dismissing any suspicions, leads or evidence I have on orders directly from you." Jackson pulled a scrunched-up piece of paper from his back pocket and laid it out as flat as he could on the desk, smoothing it over with his hand.

All through this, Cox kept his eyes on Jackson's, refusing to look at what he had placed on the desk. The two men stared at one another for a moment, before Jackson finally accepted Cox wasn't going to look, "This is a promotional poster for the 'Southumberland-Wald Forest Halloween Tour' which is travelling across Trexham and Tornwich this month. Then it's re-branding as the 'Southumberland Horror Tour' after Halloween – tonight – and travelling across the entire county."

Again, Cox said nothing and did nothing to show any sign of interest in what Jackson was telling and showing him, keeping his gaze firmly locked on Jackson's dark, brown eyes.

"The first part of the tour was held in the town of Trexham, sir, on the other side of Wald Forest. The date of the event obviously matches the date of the murders – the victims were attending the event. The second part of the tour is here in Tornwich tonight, sir, and there will be a huge crowd. It is Halloween, after all. Please let us have just a few officers and maybe a detective who is on the case, me if I have to, with them to keep an eye on things."

"Jackson, no, you're wrong." Cox stood from his seat and started putting his black uniform jacket on, "I've been working here long enough to know when an officer or detective makes a far-fetched connection to a murder and something else. This fairground tour thing," Cox waved his hand dismissively again at the poster Jackson had placed on his desk, "is simply a coincidence and will draw you away from the killer."

"Just an officer or two, please. I will go along to organise. This killer could be travelling and all I want to do is make sure more murders don't happen and to catch the sick, twisted bastard who did it if I can." His voice trembled and rose as he pleaded, betraying the anger and passion he was feeling.

Cox casually lifted his cap from his desk and placed it on his head, shoving it far enough down so that it cast a dark shadow across the top half of his face, hiding his eyes. He turned to Jackson, the only visible feature of his face now his mouth, "What exactly do you think is happening, Jackson? Some maniac clown is running around and killing people?" Cox smirked, lifting one corner of his mouth up arrogantly, giving his face even more wrinkles; despite his aging features, however, he looked very intimidating. He chuckled slightly, "Better yet, do you think the 'Bunny-Man' is back?!"

Cox walked forward, attempting to leave the room, but Jackson quickly stood and blocked his path to the doorway.

"The papers are saying it is 'The Bunny-Man', yes, sir, or a copycat. I wouldn't rule it out, I've seen strange cases here as a detective. People are frightened, the people of Southumberland have seen enough horrors over the decades, especially Trexham and here in our city. I just want to protect them, make them feel safe, give them assurance that we're there and watching out for them."

"You weren't here for all of those 'horrors' Jackson. You've been here, what is it now, seven years?"

"Yes, sir."

"Well I've been here since the very beginning." Cox sniffed.

The beginning?

"I've seen every one of them." Cox continued, "I have thirty years' experience over you, Jackson, and I am telling you right now that you are wrong."

"But the bodies were found quite close to where the attraction had been too – inside the trees of Wald Forest; I have maps on my desk and-"

"As I understand it the bodies were found almost half a mile away from where the attraction was being held. Wald Forest is a large place, I guarantee not only the people on this 'tour' would have visited the forest that night. The three who were murdered could have wandered away from the tour, gone for a walk, and then unfortunately came across the person who did this. I've done my research on this case, too, Jackson. Do not think this is some sort of personal grudge against you. If you pursue this," Cox began as he walked closer to Jackson, "I will make sure you are off this case and onto another one quicker than you can *say* Bunny-Man, do I make myself clear?" Cox's shadowed face was now only centimetres away from Jackson's.

Cox stood upright, taking his face away from Jackson's, and awaited his response.

"I will go there myself tonight if I have to," Jackson defiantly stated, "and I will prove-"

"Yourself wrong?" Cox smirked again, and from the angle Jackson was at he could now see the glimmer of Cox's icy gaze through the shadow of his cap, "and when you do, I will make sure you are punished for disobeying a direct order. Understood? That's twice I'm warning you Jackson. There will not be a third time."

With that, Cox, with one arm, shoved Jackson to one side. Jackson was too surprised by the old man's strength to respond. *This guy has got to be in his sixties and is stronger than me*, his mind screamed at him, as though calling him weak and inferior.

"If you'll excuse me," Cox mockingly began as he turned to face Jackson again, "I have a meeting with the Chief Constable and the Mayor to discuss security tonight. You see? We are protecting the people. Happy Halloween, Sergeant." Cox added sarcastically and turned back again, ducking slightly as he walked out the office doorway.

Jackson watched him leave and heard the door slam.

"Racist bastard," Jackson muttered under his breath.

Jackson picked up his poster from the desk and left the office. He noticed Cox's towering figure at the end of the hallway, near the elevator. He was talking to D.I. Hughes. *Probably giving him the latest on what we just discussed.* Everyone was scared of Cox and did as he ordered. Over the last few years, since Jackson had arrived here, Cox had been rising through the ranks of the Southumberland Constabulary. He was almost in charge now, only one step away, and everyone knew he was prepared to go to any lengths in order to snatch the Chief Constable's job for himself. He would get it anytime soon, too. Cox always got his way, through fear or through force or any other underhanded tactic he had to use.

Just a few years into Jackson's time with Southumberland Constabulary, Cox (then a Chief Superintendent) made himself seem personally responsible for a massive crackdown on the 'T-Rex' biker gang, so named because its operations mostly took place in the town of Trexham. The gang had been expanding its territory, moving certain activities and recruiting new members in Tornwich. Cox, somehow, knew where to locate the bulk of their operations and was widely credited in the media for a drug raid which saw the main leaders of the gang imprisoned. With much of their income crushed and their leaders gone, the gang was crippled. It was the huge success of that investigation, which gained national coverage, that landed Cox the job of Deputy Chief Constable. However, it was not long afterwards that two officers who had been part of that investigation were shot and killed in what was labelled a retaliation of the remnants of the T-Rex gang against the Southumberland police. It was in no doubt that the T-Rex gang had carried out the murders, but what remained unanswered was under whose command they did it. Maybe, Jackson often considered, those two officers knew how Cox had such reliable and detailed information on the T-Rex biker gang and their operations; and that the information they had would not have been as media-friendly towards him as the crackdown was.

The gang had been revived in the last few years under the influence of an American woman who the police had been investigating. However, she and her boyfriend disappeared over the summer along with a pub owner and mechanic in unexplained and mysterious circumstances, leaving the gang to rebuild once again. Jackson had thought it just as well – with the T-Rex gang seemingly under some influence from Cox, he wasn't sure how much longer the

Chief Constable would have been safe. Cox had been waiting a long time, after all.

Jackson knew his defiance was dangerous and that Cox would not take kindly to it – he was not a man who was used to such rebellious attitudes. Although his entire career was in jeopardy, Jackson wasn't going to give up on his theory.

He tried to think of the reason why Cox was so reluctant to allow him to pursue his suspicions, and came up with two possible explanations.

Either Cox simply didn't like him because he was so racist, or he was hiding something.

Or someone.

*

Chloe Clarke shuffled backwards on her bed, and was about to place her bright, white laptop on her belly before stopping herself, deciding it was better not to. Instead, she moved onto her side and put the laptop on top of the blanket.

All of her friends and family on social media were still talking about and sharing online newspaper articles about the murder of three teenagers that took place in Trexham the week before. Even though they lived in Tornwich, Trexham neighboured the city and the two shared a local bond (and rivalry most of the time, especially when it came to the local football derby and she had to put up with her boyfriend Connor and her Dad screaming and shouting at the TV or going drinking up the pub and coming back talking about the fights there had nearly been or sometimes had been). Nevertheless, Tornwich had been gripped by the same fear that Trexham had after the murders. Although there had also been a sense of unity and solidarity, terror was winning, and many people were going out less and less, many more refusing to travel through the place where the bodies had been found – Wald Forest, which usually acted as the normal route when travelling between the small town and the large city.

Chloe opened one of the online newspaper articles – the one which had been shared most on social media, the article which broke the news of the murders. It was from 'The Southumberland Gazette' and was titled: 'The New Bunny-Man?'. The article reported on how there had been no recorded 'sightings' of the Bunny-Man for almost two decades, but that it seemed the old urban legend had returned again in the style of a copycat killer to terrorise the town once more.

The three teenagers who had been murdered were all around Chloe's age – seventeen. The one girl and two boys had been part of a group of almost ten college friends who had been attending the 'Southumberland-Wald Forest Halloween Tour', and at some point were disconnected from their large group of friends and never returned. Southumberland police ruled out the possibility of there being any connection between the murders and the tour and reassured people who were going to attend the second part of the tour by saying police security in and around the event would be reviewed and strengthened.

The second part of the tour was being held on Halloween – tonight. It was being set up in Tornwich – here.

The article was vague about what the three had been put through that night, simply stating they had suffered a 'significant amount of abuse' before being murdered with an axe. This weapon, as well as the location, is what led people to draw comparisons between these murders and the urban legend of the 'Bunny-Man', who is always depicted in the local, scary tales as wielding an axe.

Police had apparently questioned workers at the event, but treated them only as 'potential witnesses', and had urged anyone who had attended the event and who thought that they may have seen anything suspicious to please 'come forward'.

Almost every comment on social media that Chloe saw was people paying tribute to those who had been murdered, but most people were also urging the people who lived in Trexham and Tornwich to go about their business as normal – including attending the second night of the Halloween tour. Very few people took to social media to voice their fear, whether it be over the second night of the tour or just going out in general; these concerns were only spoken – hushed – in private.

Beep, beep.

Chloe's thoughts had become so entangled with the local tragedy that she almost jumped out of her skin when her phone started ringing.

Beep, beep.

She didn't answer straight away – she had to calm her nerves first otherwise her voice would sound suspiciously shaky.

Beep, beep.

She grabbed her phone from off the bedside table, looked at the name, took a deep, strained breath and answered.

"Sarah?" She managed, and coughed afterwards to get rid of the tremour of tension in her voice.

"Chloe! You doing anything tonight?"

"Erm…" She thought for a moment, but her mind was blank, she hadn't fully composed herself from the scare her phone had given her.

"You and Connor going to dress up in some sexy Halloween costumes and have a night of frightening passion?" Sarah laughed.

"Sarah!"

She laughed again, relieving the tension, bringing Chloe's memory back.

"There's a gathering at someone's house – can't remember if it was at Nan's or Auntie's – but I think I was just going to go there and help some of the little cousins go trick or treating."

"Sounds shit." Sarah bluntly stated.

"Tell me about it." Chloe agreed, before feeling a little guilty, "I'm sure it won't be so bad… It can be nice when the family is all together sometimes."

"Well, anyway, don't worry about that."

"Why? What are your plans?"

The response hit Chloe harder than she ever thought it would. What Sarah proposed was not something she had considered, even thought was a possibility, but Sarah's words made it become a horrifying reality.

"Me and Josh were thinking about going to that Wald Forest Halloween tour, would be fun if you and Connor joined us."

Chloe didn't respond – she couldn't.

"It sounds fun," Sarah continued, "There's a regular fairground there and some 'horror mazes'. Have a look at the website, show Connor, and let me know in a bit. Okay?"

"Yeah, sounds good." Chloe said, finally having regained her ability to speak.

She felt vulnerable, she realised everything was scaring her far too easily, she wanted Connor to be there with her.

Why am I so scared?

"I'll speak to you later-"

"Aren't you scared though?" Chloe blurted out before Sarah had a chance to hang up.

"Scared?" Sarah sought clarification.

"The murders in Trexham the other week… Those people were at this tour."

Sarah laughed, "Oh, Chloe! Don't be stupid. It's fine. Police said there's no connection and they've maxed-out security at tonight's event. And listen, even if there is a link, the killer would be an idiot to strike in the same place again wouldn't he? Police will be on anything suspicious tonight in seconds."

"It's Halloween," Chloe responded, "People are walking around covered in fake blood, dressed up as killers, what's suspicious? A killer would blend in well."

"Chloe. Chill the fuck out. Let me know what you're doing tonight, okay?"

"Okay, I'll talk to Connor."

"See you later!"

Chloe took the phone away from her ear.

Sarah's attitude had actually comforted her slightly. She had already assumed that she and Connor would be going with them, which was strangely calming. Sarah was acting as though there was nothing to worry about, and Chloe knew there probably wasn't, she was just being cautious.

Turning her focus back to her laptop, Chloe searched for the tour online. The aptly decorated website was dark, framed by cobwebs, written in a red, blood-like font. The information provided was exactly as Sarah had described it over the phone: a fairground accompanied three 'horror mazes'. Very little detail was given as to what the mazes contained, but after Chloe found some blogs of people who had visited the first night of the tour, she discovered they were attractions which groups walked through as they were terrorised by actors, horror film style sets and special effects.

It does sound quite fun.

Chloe picked up her phone once again and text Connor, telling him about Sarah's suggestion for that night. She knew it was very unlikely that he wouldn't want to go. She wouldn't argue, she *did* want to go herself now. But still there was mild apprehension inside of her. She would go and try to enjoy herself, but in the back of her mind would be the murders from earlier that month, and she would probably be keeping a close eye on everyone that night.

Beep, beep.

Chloe almost threw her laptop off the bed when her phone started ringing again.

Fucking calm down!

"Hi babe," Connor's voice spoke, "I'm up for tonight with Sarah and Josh, but aren't your family going to be pissed if we aren't with them?"

"They did invite us…" Chloe said thoughtfully, considering their options, "But if we go there for an hour or two until the start of the event tonight then it should be okay."

"Sounds good to me, what time are they all getting together?"

"Probably around five."

"Cool, I'll get to you just before that then." There was a silence for a few moments, before Connor finally asked, "I didn't think this is something you'd want to do, after what happened the other week."

"I am still scared… But I've just been reading about how much police they're sending tonight, we'll be safe."

"Good," Connor sighed, satisfied, "We can't be scared of them."

"I know." Chloe sighed.

But then she remembered something.

She shouldn't be going to the horror tour at all, for a completely different reason than fear. It wasn't suitable for someone in her condition; the rides, the mazes wouldn't be safe for exactly the same reason she'd stopped putting her laptop on her belly.

She was pregnant.

*

He sat in front of the mirror and stared at himself.

He checked his phone. Still over seven hours to go.

He didn't want to wait that long, he wanted to start getting ready *now*.

Pat, pat, pat.

He looked around, thinking someone was knocking at the tent, but when he saw the dark circles and drips falling against the light blue surface he understood that it was raining.

Only spitting, he thanked the sky; it meant he wouldn't have to re-do his face paint later. He probably would anyway, though, or at least perfect it shortly before the start of that night's event.

Slowly and carefully, he reached for the small, black bag behind the mirror containing his face paints and make-up. He unzipped it, and took out the small see-through tub that was smudged white.

Slowly and carefully, he applied it to his face. Going over and over his face again and again, rubbing layer after layer of the substance into his face, fastidiously working to ensure that every square millimetre of the skin from his throat upwards was completely white.

Slowly and carefully, he played back each moment of the last time. The group he had stalked throughout the night, watching them closely and picking out his preferred victims.

The girl, she'd been one of his picks. The two males had just been close by her, making it easy to catch them, and he'd recognised them as part of the group too. They had served him just as well as she had in the end, though.

Patpatpatpatpatpatpatpat.

Shit.

Doesn't matter.

He carried on applying the white paint to his face, watching the movements of his face in the mirror as he did so. How his light, pale skin became paler, eventually lightening into complete whiteness. His bright, blue eyes gleamed at his features; his smooth, clean skin, his thin neck making his jawline look strong and firm, his black hair messy and shooting wildly in every direction.

He placed the lid back on the tub of white face paint and put it back into the small, black bag, then shuffling his long, thin fingers around in the bag, identifying the shape of what he required, he drew out a shiny gold coloured cylinder which with a slow and deliberate twist of his hands revealed itself to be a bright red lipstick.

He had tested red face paint before the first night of the tour and hadn't liked it. He had found that lipstick worked much better. It was brighter, more visible, more precise. He liked his face to be perfect.

Slowly and carefully, he applied the lipstick only to his lips, making sure none of it got onto his face.

Then, he substituted the lipstick for a tub of black face paint, using that to only slightly smudge underneath his eyes.

In his opinion, the face being almost completely white with little colour was more frightening.

Maybe later he would experiment, wash his face and test an all-white look.

But would that go with his costume?

He would experiment. There were still hours to kill, after all.

Next, he reached behind the mirror once again and pulled out a hairbrush. He began combing his hair forwards; slowly and carefully, every movement practiced and precise, every part of the act of preparation adding to the enjoyment of his ritual; before parting it on the left side, sweeping the rest of it to the right and then brushing the right side of his hair backwards.

He also brushed his sideburns (which came right the way down to his jawline) backwards slightly to neaten them up.

He set his brush and black bag to one side, and stared at himself in the mirror again.

"Perfect," He whispered, "You look perfect."

Concentrating, he realised he'd lost track of time and had almost forgotten about the excitement he would be experiencing that night, this was merely the entrée, but what point an entrée if there is no main course he chuckled to himself?

He checked his phone, six and a half hours to go.

Yes, he would experiment some more with his appearance.

Pat, pat, pat.

Slowly and carefully, he turned his head.

He looked at the headline of the folded newspaper in the far corner of the tent: 'The New Bunny-Man?'

On top of the newspaper rested his axe.

Chapter Two

It was nearing four o'clock, and Jackson knew that soon he would be leaving the station and heading towards Wald Forest. It was about a ten, fifteen minute drive depending on traffic. The event wouldn't be opening until about seven, and despite Jackson knowing from experience that any potential incidents at an event were likely to occur late in the night rather than early on, he wanted to get there as soon as possible just to keep an eye out for anything suspicious.

Cox had claimed security and policing was being reviewed and strengthened, but Jackson knew that if he was so worried about him going to the event, Cox would find a way to make sure heads were turned the other way and security that night would be made as lax as possible so that whatever he's hiding isn't found out.

He set his computer to shut down, and watching the bright blue screen fade swiftly into blackness made him think of sleep. He was so tired, and yet could not slip into the sweet oblivion of sleep. He hadn't been able to sleep last night, and knew without even trying that tonight would be even worse. He *had* to go to the tour, he *had* to prove that his theory was right, he *had* to take Cox down.

Since his conversation with Deputy Chief Constable Cox that afternoon, he had convinced himself that Cox was somehow involved in the murders, and that catching the killer would mean seeing justice brought upon Cox too.

Jackson caught a glimpse of himself in the blackness of his computer monitor. His eyes were beginning to sag badly, and beads of sweat were already running down his bald head. He rubbed a hand through his bushy, black beard as he yawned, and then wiped a hand over his head as he stood up from his desk.

He tucked his shirt into his trousers and tightened his belt. Bending down, he retrieved something from underneath his desk that he always kept hidden in a cardboard box beneath piles of papers and folders. He flung the covert harness over one shoulder, and then the other, before straightening out his shirt and tucking it in neatly once again. The harness held all the necessities he required for nights like this; handcuffs, baton, pepper spray – all of which he kept locked away in the top drawer of his desk.

It wasn't the norm for detectives to wear a belt or harness with police equipment on it – but Jackson often opted to use one when he felt he would need it, especially on nights like tonight, when there was a big chance of getting into a struggle or a fight. He wasn't exactly planning to be totally undercover, he wanted visitors and staff at the event to know there was police presence, so saw more benefits in wearing it than not.

Then, Detective Sergeant James Jackson rolled his light blue shirt sleeves up to just above his elbows, buttoned them, picked up his Tornwich United football hoodie and exited his office to the hallway. As Jackson was walking down a flight of stairs, zipping up his hoodie, he was brought to a sudden stop by a figure blocking his path.

Jackson's first, panicked thought, was that Cox had sent someone to silence him. But as Jackson readied for a struggle, he saw a face that he recognised and had not seen in a long time.

"Andy?" Jackson questioned his own eyes aloud.

The response he got was a hug, to which he was at first shocked, but eventually returned the gesture.

"I didn't think you were coming back," Jackson commented, "It's been so long. I'd heard you'd moved away."

"I went on... what we'll call a 'long holiday', JJ, but I didn't move. I always wanted to come back. It's taken a lot longer than I wanted, but yeah, I'm back now." Andy smiled. "Still supporting the scum I see?" Andy broke the silence that hung in the air for a few seconds after he had declared his return, laughed, and patted the Tornwich United logo on Jackson's hoodie.

"Unfortunately," Jackson sighed, "But hey! We nearly got promoted last season, didn't we? And you nearly went down."

"Ah, but now *you're* rock bottom of the table, two months in and not even in double figures in terms of points yet. I reckon we knocked your confidence with that draw at the end of last season to keep you down with us. How the tables turn." Andy smiled slyly.

"Bastards," Jackson retorted.

"You're investigating the axe murders?" The tone of Andy's voice dropped as suddenly as the smile on his face.

Jackson nodded.

"I won't keep you." Andy said, and patted Jackson on the shoulder, "I'm sure I'll be seeing you later in the week, anyway."

"Yeah. Good to see you again, Andy."

"You too, JJ. We'll have a catch-up drink the weekend or something."

The men exchanged nods of the head and continued walking in opposite directions.

Andy seemed like his normal self to Jackson, and acted as though he'd been back at work for a while. Andy was often based in Trexham and spent only a little time in Tornwich depending on what case he was assigned to. Last summer, Andy was one of the officers called to the scene of a horrific massacre at Southumberland Zoo. A schoolboy had turned on his fellow students, according to the local and national news reports, and it was reported he used knives to mutilate several of his classmates before disappearing into Wald Forest.

This is what the media were told; the police were told differently by the few surviving witnesses.

Unfortunately, social media somehow got hold of this information (as it always seemed to these days), and this led to the event becoming known as Trexham's 'Full Moon' Prom. These reports remained unconfirmed, and the sinister schoolboy – Kevin Baxter – remained missing to this day.

*

Chloe leaned forward and quickly glanced around out of her bedroom window.

No sign of Connor yet.

It was just after four o'clock, so he should probably be getting to her soon. They had agreed to spend a few hours at the family Halloween party, and that started at five, and then they would probably be heading to the horror tour with Sarah and Josh when it opened at seven.

Chloe relaxed again on her bed and distracted herself by tapping away on her phone, scrolling through social media and occasionally opening a game to try and kill more time.

She had been with Connor for a little over a year now, and yet still felt the same pangs of excitement whenever she knew that he was coming to see her.

He was one of the first people she had met at college – they sat next to one another after being placed in the same tutor group. So when the tutor ran through the usual introductory and 'ice-breaker' tasks, which Chloe (and most other students) loathed, she was surprised to find that she felt comfortable and happy talking to the handsome boy who had sat next to her.

For the rest of that first week of college, Chloe found herself constantly looking forward to having tutorials. Which, thankfully for her, they had every day that week because it was the college's induction week.

Every day she would sit staring at him, especially when the tutor was talking. She admired his short, blond hair and his light stubble, and loved to look into his bright, blue eyes whenever he was talking to her.

She didn't tell anyone about the feelings she had developed for him, but one day when he walked past her and her group of friends, he waved. Innocent and friendly at first, she returned the gesture, only to turn back to her friends who had somehow seen how she felt about him; as though her pupils had turned into love-hearts the moment she looked at him. She had to admit, the way her belly filled with butterflies and her head went light, it felt as though her eyes did turn to love-hearts when she saw him. It was like the rest of the world suddenly became non-existent whenever he was near. Her friends saw this, mocked her about it as friends did, and she strongly denied what they were saying as people often do when being accused of liking someone.

Even though she didn't admit it, the conversation ended with Chloe pleading with her friends not to say anything. They turned away from the mockery and pledged not to. Afterwards, one of the friends spoke to Chloe in their English lesson, and Chloe felt it was very relaxing to unload her feelings onto someone who was willing to listen and keep what she had said secret. That friend, as it turned out, also had feelings for a boy at college and confided in Chloe. The boy was called Josh, and the friend was Sarah.

Chloe left the comfort of her bed and sat down at her desk on the other side of the room. She tilted her small, circular mirror downwards slightly so she could see her face fully. She had already done her hair and make-up earlier, but she just wanted to make sure that she still looked as good as she could for Connor's arrival.

She reached into one of her drawers, pulled out a comb, and began neatening her shoulder-length blonde hair.

It was the second week of college which had seen Sarah and Josh begin a relationship, shortly followed by Chloe and Connor. Early on in the week in an English lesson, Sarah had turned up excitedly telling Chloe about how Josh had kissed her that morning in the college café.

"Just out of the blue and in front of everyone?" Chloe had questioned, slightly amused by the image that had formed in her mind of Josh just grabbing Sarah and pushing their faces against one another's in front of a stunned audience.

"No!" Sarah had responded defensively, "It was quite empty and nobody was looking. Besides, it wasn't a big kiss... Just... Short and sweet." Sarah had said and smiled like an infatuated schoolgirl. "We were just talking about our law work and he suddenly put his face really close to mine. I didn't back away and so he just... kissed me!"

Chloe remembered being happy and pleased that Sarah had got what she wanted, but it also made her more aware that she had made no progress with Connor and made her feel as though she wasn't going to.

So, she was entirely lost for words to see Connor waiting for her after that English lesson had finished.

He said hello to her, and she smiled back, thinking he must have been waiting for another friend in the lesson. However, she was happily shocked when he started walking alongside her. When they left the building, they stood and faced one another, waiting to see who would be first to say goodbye. For a moment, Chloe had thought they would just turn and walk away, but Connor took a step closer to her and bent down slightly. Chloe, almost without thinking, lunged forward and quickly kissed him. She pulled back to see his reaction, and saw the delight in his eyes.

After that, they had shared a longer kiss.

Knock, knock, knock.

Chloe took one last look at herself in the mirror.

Her hair was sufficiently neat, her green eyes were sufficiently bright, her face sufficiently colourful, her lips sufficiently... *kissable*? She hoped so.

She stood, pulled her light blue jeans up, her black, long-sleeved shirt down slightly, and bounded down the stairs.

"Your parents already at the party?" Connor asked as he rushed inside, the door barely opened.

"Yeah." Chloe replied, and was then suddenly being pulled towards Connor and being kissed eagerly.

He pulled away, took her hand and rushed up the stairs.

He tugged at her shirt as she reclined on the bed and she took it off for him as he took his off.

"You've been playing football?" She asked, just noticing he was wearing his Tornwich United football kit for the first time.

"Well, these aren't my everyday clothes are they?" He responded sarcastically, smiling, showing off his neat, white teeth.

"Well, Connor, I didn't have much time to look at you before you launched at me you sex pest." She hit back.

"Didn't see you complaining." He smiled again and kneeled on the bed.

She put a hand on his chest, feeling the firmness of his muscles and stroking the light, blond hairs across them.

She backed up on the bed some more, and unzipped her jeans as Connor pulled down his shorts.

"I love you," She smiled up at him, with the same butterflies in her belly as were there the first time she saw him.

"I love you too," He said, and leaned over her, and as happened every time she looked at him, she fell in love all over again.

*

After the things Jackson had heard about the night of the 'Full Moon' Prom, he was surprised Andy had returned to work at all.

Jackson was thankful he had been on another case at the time, for he feared witnessing the horrors he had only been told about would have also ended his career as it had so many others.

Thinking about what Andy and other officers must have been through that night made Jackson remember the bodies of the three teenagers he had seen almost two weeks ago.

The images of the three bodies kept flashing in Jackson's mind.

They had been haunting him in his nightmares too, in the few hours of sleep he'd managed to get since then.

He must have seen dozens of dead bodies while working for the police in Southumberland, but none had hit him as hard as the axed teenagers in Trexham.

It was the horror they had been through.

They hadn't just been murdered; they'd all been sexually abused in one way or another – including the males, and their bodies had been put through what Jackson imagined must have been horrendous and excruciating pain.

The grotesque memory of the girl was the worst for Jackson; her face had been split open with an axe. The wound was so large that she had no facial features remaining. All that was left was a bulging, red mess – something that reminded Jackson of an erupted volcano.

Jackson could think of only one word to describe how the two males met their end: butchered. The axe had not been used on their heads, but had been used to almost decapitate one of them, leaving the head hanging on by thin layers of skin. Jackson, however, knew that this had been the fatal blow. Before that, the killer had inflicted a tremendous amount of damage with his axe all across the man's body. The other male… he had actually been completely dismembered.

Jackson knew the tour was a cover for the killer. Hughes knew it, the other detectives knew it, and most of all, Cox knew it. *Why is Cox protecting such a twisted killer?*

Jackson tried to think of any links the three teenagers could have to Cox, and any reasons Cox could have to want them killed, but this didn't fit Cox's MO in terms of making his enemies and threats to his position disappear. This had the feel of a serial killer about it, one just starting to find his rhythm, and Jackson had to stop him. *So why has Cox been so reluctant to let me pursue this? He's a corrupt bastard, only out for himself, but he doesn't unnecessarily delay investigations. What is in this for him?*

Jackson's mind was racing with possible explanations, and his thoughts even tried to tell him that Cox was the murderer, but that didn't make sense either. Cox was more of a calculated gangster, not a psychopathic killer.

Jackson had been walking through the trees of Wald Forest for almost two hours now, and had come across nothing. It would probably take a team of officers just a matter of hours to search the important parts of the forest that surrounded Tornwich, but that was a privilege Jackson couldn't exercise thanks to Cox, and it would probably take Jackson days to cover the maze of trees around the city – it *was* one of the largest forests in Britain.

Sergeant Jackson had decided not to head straight to the tour event from the station, after all. Instead, he had driven along some of the perimeter of the forest, occasionally parking his car to go through the trees on foot. He had found nothing. No stalkers or strange people lurking around, just the normal, everyday locals using the woodland to ride their bikes, jog through or walk their dogs.

Jackson decided he had wasted enough time trying to find anything inside the towering trees of the forest, and that now it was nearly six o'clock, he should probably head to the event itself.

He left the woodland and got into his car.

He took a deep breath and scanned the trees one last time.

He had no idea of the terror he would witness inside them later that night.

*

Lincoln Brooks couldn't believe his luck. He had been nervous about bringing it up to his friends, but as soon as he had they'd been just as up for it as he was. However, he knew that they didn't want to go for the same reasons as him. They saw tonight as an opportunity to hang out, drink and have fun getting scared. Not that Lincoln didn't enjoy those things too, but his main reason for being there was one he couldn't share.

Not because it was sinister. Nothing like that. It's just that he'd experienced… *troubles* in the past with his… *interests*.

But that didn't matter now, anyway. He had gotten what he wanted and he and his friends were now on their way to the 'Southumberland-Wald Forest Halloween Tour'.

"So what made you think of this, Lincoln?" One of his friends asked as they walked through the city centre which was like a forest of its own; towering shops surrounding them, reaching up towards the dark night sky and blocking most of it out.

Lincoln swallowed and felt his heart rate increase slightly. The questions. He didn't want the questions. That's how it had all started before. In school…

"I… Erm…" He took in a breath and tried to steady his voice, "Just saw some posters for it. I thought it would be a good thing for us to do before we had to go back to college." He let the breath escape, it exited his nostrils shakily.

"Well, it was a good idea." Came the reply, and Lincoln smiled as he felt his muscles relax, "We needed one last meet-up before going back to college, anyway."

Lincoln nodded. He was in his second year at college and was going to university next year. He was going to be living there while he studied sports, but wouldn't really be leaving home; he was going to the University of Tornwich.

He was interested in sports. He'd always watched football with his Dad and played it with his friends, but it wasn't what he wanted to study. In a part of him, deep inside his mind, he'd hidden his true interests and desires away long ago.

"Does anyone know where we're going?" Another of the group asked.

"Follow the signs." Lincoln said, and pointed to a large poster outside a shop that told all 'victims visitors of the Halloween Tour to follow the arrows', which pointed straight ahead.

"We're going to get lost." One of the girls tutted.

Lincoln knew that they didn't have to walk much further before employees of the attraction appeared to start directing them into Wald Forest where the tour was being held – he'd read so on the website. But he didn't say anything, he couldn't. Or they would suspect, and then they would know. Just like in school…

He pushed the memories back, as he always did, burying them away in the past where they belonged

But still, the desire to do something different with his life always remained. Sports had been an interest, a hobby, but he didn't want it to dominate his life. He'd had to allow it to, though. It was the only way to mask his true self from everyone else. People just didn't understand, and they would never understand. He would be treated differently. He *had* to fit in. Sports had been what he'd turned to in order to do that. It was easy, seeing as it was already something he liked.

Not only had he turned to sports, but used that to change something else about his lifestyle. Towards the end of high school, he had started going to the gym. By the time he started college, he had completely transformed himself. Through school, he had been quiet and skinny. Now in college, he was popular and muscular.

But still, in the privacy of his own bedroom, he allowed himself to look at the things that interested him the most. That was how he really came across the 'Southumberland-Wald Forest Halloween Tour'.

One night, like so many nights, sat alone in his room. In the dark. Lincoln would take interest in what most people found weird. He would research cases, join blogs, read books, make notes and write works and theories of his own around the subject – always making him wish he'd followed his heart and studied what he really wanted to at college and, soon, at university: psychology, criminology, the things that really interested him.

But he had chosen his path. Now his other interests were confined to the shadows of his bedroom – even his books on the world's most famous serial killers, his favourite collection, hidden away in his drawers or in boxes underneath his bed. His shelves occupied with autobiographies of his favourite football players and managers as well as sports and fitness magazines.

Stemming from his interest in killers, like Jack the Ripper, was an interest in all sorts of spooky things. Which is why he often considered himself lucky that he was born in

Tornwich, near the forest that was home to the urban legend of the 'Bunny-Man Bridge'.

*

"See you later, Mom."

"You're going already?" Chloe's Mom asked, surprised, as she looked up at her.

"Yeah, Sarah and Josh will be here in a minute, we're heading over soon."

"Okay, love," Her Mom held her arms out and Chloe leaned into her hug, "Make sure you're careful."

"I will," Chloe said.

When Chloe stood again she was met from a flood of 'goodbye' and 'have fun' comments from family members and friends who were seated in the surrounding area. Connor also hugged her Mom and said goodbye to everyone who was nearby.

Then, as quickly as they could, Chloe and Connor shuffled through the crowds of family members and friends gathered in the rooms and hallways of her Auntie's house nodding and smiling without directly saying goodbye to anyone else; Chloe had just wanted to make sure she said bye to her Mom, otherwise leaving the house would have probably taken hours with the amount of family members that were there.

But her plan of a swift exit failed; it had been wishful thinking that she could get out of the house unnoticed by the dozens of family members packed into the rooms and hallways not large enough to contain them all.Chloe wouldn't have been too annoyed having to say goodbye to most family members, but the one who stood in her and Connor's path meant that she had to stop herself from sighing aloud and rolling her eyes in irritation.

Uncle Des. Not related by blood – he was married to her Auntie (one on her Father's side, not the one whose house they were in). Actually, when she thought of it, that made this encounter all the more strange. Why was he even here? Tonight's gathering was mostly her Mother's side of the family.

Chloe tried to make eye contact with Connor, only to realise that he was already walking out of the front door. Uncle Des had positioned himself in such a way where he'd blocked Chloe's path, but not Connor's; meaning Connor probably hadn't noticed and was now headed for the front garden to wait for Sarah and Josh. *Shit.*

"You're leaving are you?" He asked in a voice that, as ever, was barely audible. The groups of people talking around them made it even more difficult to hear him. If she hadn't lip read the last two words she wouldn't have understood the question in its entirety. She almost shivered. 'You're leaving?' would have been perfectly normal, but the two words added onto the end made the question sound like an accusation. Or, more terrifyingly, a threat.

She nodded and managed a little smile, "Yeah, see you soon." She spoke as she tried to step around him, but he followed her path, blocking it once again.

"I don't see enough of you these days." He commented, and through the thick lenses of his glasses she saw that his eyes dropped slightly, before quickly he forced them to look up again. "Are you going to that horror thing tonight?" He tried to sound casual, but as usual his words were forced; he never sounded like a normal human, more like a robot.

She nodded again, and then once more tried to manoeuvre herself around him, even if she could just get to the front door to try and shout Connor…

Uncle Des' hand fell on her shoulder and she tried her best not to recoil in horror and disgust. He stepped a little too close to her, so close that she could smell the alcohol on his breath. "Maybe I'll see you there." He smiled, his lips curling upwards at first, then parting to show his teeth.

"Des." A shoulder grabbed hold of her Uncle's shoulder, the fingers turning white. Chloe recognised the fingers as Connor's. Uncle Des took a step backwards, but the way he did so let Chloe know that it had been reluctant – Connor had pulled him back rather than Des stepping away of his own accord.

"Coming, Chloe?" Connor looked at her, all the while still keeping a firm grip on Des' shoulder.

"Des!" Chloe turned and saw that at the end of the hallway her Auntie – Des' wife – was calling him over. She saw him give Connor an annoyed and angry look before walking off down the hallway. So they were here together, after all, Uncle Des hadn't just invited himself.

"You okay?" Connor asked, putting his arm around her and leading her out of the front door.

"Yeah, he's just *so* creepy. I don't even think he realises what he's doing."

"You really should tell your Mom about him. Your Dad, even."

"They both know what he's like. We all try and avoid him whenever possible. God knows what my Auntie sees in him – she sees less of the entire family because of him. It's weird they even got invited tonight."

"God. Fucking weirdo. I'll knock him out if he ever comes near you again."

Chloe smiled a little before hiding it, "Please don't cause a family war. I can't handle it."

He laughed.

When they got to the front garden it was empty.

"Where are they?" Connor asked.

"They should be here by now…" Chloe said, and walked out of the garden and looked down both sides of the street.

Connor came up behind Chloe, put his arms around her and rested his chin on her head.

He had changed clothes after arriving at her house, putting on some jeans and a black jumper; an outfit almost matching her own, except Chloe was now wearing a puffy white coat (which she had put on after feeling how cold it was outside) that now covered her black shirt.

Suddenly, bright lights appeared on the road and then swiftly turned towards Chloe and Connor, momentarily blinding them until they were shut off.

"Oh, looks like Josh drove." Chloe commented, "Come on."

They both walked around either side of the car and climbed onto the back seats.

"Evening gang," Josh said.

"Everyone excited?" Sarah asked.

"Oh, yeah." Connor said, "Couldn't get much detail on what's there, though."

Chloe had decided she had no choice to go to the event unless she was going to tell everyone she was pregnant, and she wasn't prepared to do that yet; it was still early. She was going to try and go on only tame rides at the fairground part of the attraction and make a judgement on the 'horror mazes' when she got there.

She would feign illness if she had to, and if she *really* had to, she supposed she would break the news to Connor.

"I heard there's a 'Bunny-Man Bridge' maze." Josh said, "There's some blogs online from people who went to the first night."

"Do they sound scary?" Chloe asked, and Connor reassuringly put his hand on her leg and squeezed.

"Not too bad, actually," Josh said, and Chloe relaxed slightly, "It sounds more like we walk through a set built to resemble whatever the maze is based around; so I'm guessing a 'Bunny-Man' maze would be set in the forest and have a fake bridge or something, and besides that it mostly sounds like watching actors perform scenes and try to scare us.....no touching or anything like that, obviously." He added hastily as Connor flashed him a look in the rear-view mirror.

"That sounds cool." Chloe said, and looked at Connor and smiled. He smiled back, and his eyes showed his relief that Chloe's earlier fears had now seemingly been eased.

"Where do we need to go?" Connor asked, "The forest?"

"The forest." Sarah confirmed.

"But we need to go to the city first," Josh said, "We'll be directed to where we need to go then."

Josh carried on driving until the huge shopping complex in the city centre became visible against the dark night sky.

Beyond the complex, beyond the roads and the houses was Wald Forest, which later that night would be the most terrifying maze of all.

*

Jackson started his car and began driving towards the city centre. The 'Southumberland-Wald Forest Halloween Tour' website was recommending that visitors park in the city centre and follow signs or take advice from members of staff situated throughout the city centre; either of these would lead customers to the area of Wald Forest where the second night of the tour was being held.

From the maps on the website Jackson saw that the event had found enough open space inside Wald Forest to set its attractions up.

The huge shopping complex in the city centre came into view and Jackson turned into the car park. It was already rammed with vehicles and there were groups of people clustered along the road – Jackson guessed that they were talking to members of staff from the tour and getting directions to Wald Forest.

Jackson decided that was probably the best thing for him to do, too.

He left his car, locked it and tagged onto a group huddled around a member of staff. The group appeared to be a family – parents with their teenage children. The member of staff was tall and dressed up in a cheap Halloween Dracula costume, but his stature and acting skills managed to erase the cheapness of it, and in fact he actually made himself come across as quite intimidating.

He spoke in a low, upper class drawl, giving directions to the forest where he "often comes to find blood". He crossed his arms, bringing his black cape across his entire body as he finished telling them where to go. His hair was shiny and slicked back, his face pale white with red circles painted on the corner of his lip, stretching down to his chin.

"If you come across any of my… 'assistants' in the forest," the Dracula-dressed member of staff began before they could all walk away, "be sure to mention that I sent you. That should keep you safe... for tonight." He said, displaying his over developed canines to great effect whilst annunciating the 't's. With that, he turned slowly and walked down the road and towards another group of people.

"I hope I'm not paying good bloody money for shit supermarket costumes like that all night." The man of the group who Jackson had tagged onto huffed.

"Oh, Dad, he was creepy!"

"If you say so, love. Come on, let's get going. These 'maze' things better be worth it."

Jackson began walking in the direction that the cheap-but-convincing Dracula told them to. Along the way, there were signs pinned to lamp-posts, walls and buildings to indicate which way visitors should go; there were also more costumed members of staff to ensure that people were heading in the right direction and didn't get lost.

When he finally arrived at the trees of the intimidatingly large and dark forest, he could see that booths had been set up slightly inside the darkness, just shadowed enough to be creepy, but not enough so that they weren't visible to customers.

Jackson told the young, female vampire in the booth that he was with the police and part of the security that had been sent to guard the event that night. He showed her his badge and warrant card. She seemed to hesitate for a moment, unsure of what to do, but eventually just opted for giving him a wristband, leaflet guide and wishing him a 'nightmarish night'. She also seemed hesitant to quote that line to him, obviously taking his profession and reason for being at the event into account. She wasn't as good an actor as the Dracula he'd seen earlier, but he could understand why given the fear that people sometimes felt in the presence of the police.

Upon walking past the booth, the forest path was illuminated only by small lamps strapped to trees. The night air was ice-like, and a thin fog had descended across the forest. Hordes of the undead were marching slowly and sinisterly through the trees, sniffing visitors who passed them and only slightly breaking character when unfazed or desperate customers asked which way to go – to which they would simply hang a limp arm in the right direction and then continue stomping through the forest.

Jackson walked for a few seconds until he came to a huge clearing.

It took a moment for his eyes to adjust to the incredible amount of light there now was.

First he saw the small Ferris wheel in the distance, and in his more immediate proximity were the three horror-themed maze events that he recognised from the brief glance he had given the leaflet handed to him at the entrance booths.

Jackson felt quite dazed by the bright colour and noise of the area he was now in, and decided to first head to a large, white tent, clearly and simply labelled as 'BAR', where quite a few visitors, seemingly having the same idea as him, were already heading towards as their first destination.

As Jackson had already considered, if anything was likely to happen it would be late in the night rather than early on, so he thought that he might as well try and relax a little first and get used to his surroundings instead of launching straight into investigating everything in his path.

Inside the tent was a bar, and at the other end a small platform where a band of black-cloaked, green-faced witches were performing classic Halloween songs.

Funny, Jackson thought as he leaned against the bar, *I haven't seen a single security guard or police officer yet.*

Fuck you, Cox.

*

He swung his axe through the air and brought it crashing into the side of a tree.

Whoosh.

Thud.

The only sound it lacked from hitting a person was the squishing sound that was made by the blade crushing through flesh and blood.

In the end, he had decided against an all-white face. He had tried it earlier that afternoon, but it didn't match his costume.

Instead, most of his face remained white, but there was a smudged circle around both of his eyes, and he had put red lipstick around his lips slightly as well as on them. He had also used the lipstick to paint a small circular area on the tip of his nose. When he had been applying his face-paint, an idea had struck him about something else he could add to his image. He had scooped all of the green face-paint out of its tub and using his fingers, run it through his hair and sideburns. Most of his hair remained its natural black colour, but there were green areas and spots among it. However, the sides of his hair and sideburns were mostly green.

He had also been daring in other ways that night.

He had moved his tents closer to the attraction than last time. Last time it had been a struggle taking the three people as far through the forest as they had. This time, the tents were only a few hundred metres away from the attraction.

He took his phone out of his pocket and checked the time.

Time to go to work.

He threw his axe back into his tent, and started walking through the thin fog that had descended over the trees and towards the bright lights and dense wall of noise that was 'The Southumberland-Wald Forest Halloween Tour'.

Chapter Three

Chloe held her hands out in front of her, trying to reach as far forward as she could to warm them up. Her feet felt as though they were beginning to freeze and she could barely feel her toes; she held those out in front of her as well.

She was sat on a tree stump, as were many other visitors. They were all circled around a large bonfire and almost all of them were carrying out the same actions as Chloe; holding their hands and feet out as far as they could to try and battle against the ice-cold air.

She looked to the right at the large, white tent that was serving as the makeshift pub for the event. Connor and Josh had gone in there to go and get drinks for the four of them whilst Chloe and Sarah had stayed by the large bonfire to try and get as warm as possible before they all started going into the horror mazes and fairground attractions.

Chloe looked forward and across the bonfire – towards where the fairground attractions had been set up. About two-hundred metres away, towering over everything else at the event was a Ferris wheel, which just about managed to carry people over the trees of Wald Forest at its peak. So far Chloe had also seen other traditional fairground attractions such as a Waltzer and shooting games (from which prizes could be won) scattered around the Ferris wheel. However, there didn't seem to be much at this part of the event compared to other fairgrounds Chloe had been to; it was clear this part of the tour was only secondary to all the horror-themed 'mazes'.

The maze entrances were over to the left.

Chloe had glanced at all of them upon entering the large clearing that had been found – or created – for the event. She had only taken note of one of them at first, though; it seemed to jump out at her as soon as she saw the lettering. A plastic building, made to look like stone, had been constructed to resemble a bridge – with the entrance a black archway that people were queuing at. Above this archway, in lettering which simulated dripping blood, were the words 'Bunny-Man Bridge'. The building seemed to be small, and so Chloe assumed that it was serving only as an entryway into the forest where this maze would be. The other two maze entrances were larger and not as close to the trees, so would presumably be held indoors.

Although Josh had claimed there was a 'Bunny-Man Bridge' maze at the event, seeing it had scared Chloe slightly because it reminded her of the murders in Trexham earlier that month and the links that were being made to the 'Bunny-Man' urban legend.

Chloe tried to cast those thoughts from her mind, and had turned her attention away from that maze.

The maze to the right of the replicated 'Bunny-Man Bridge' was a 'Haunted House'. It had been built to look like a house from centuries ago, and Chloe mentally placed it somewhere close to the Tudor age based on its design. From the leaflet handed to her at the entrance booths and from Josh's reading of blogs, this maze sounded the tamest in terms of 'jump scares' and actors communicating with visitors, although it sounded more atmospheric and creepy.

The final horror maze seemed out of place and as though it belonged with the fairground part of the event, but Chloe guessed it would be much different to the ride with which it shared its name.

'Ghost Train'.

*

Sergeant Jackson left the large, white tent with his plastic cup of lager and began walking towards the large bonfire in the middle of the clearing.

It seemed the night air was getting colder and colder. He could barely hold his cup in one hand for more than a few seconds because of how it made his fingers feel like they were beginning to freeze. Never being a fan of warm beer, he wouldn't have to worry about that tonight he mused to himself.

The fog in the air had stayed thin, and at times was barely visible, which would make his job that night a lot easier.

Once at the bonfire, he set his cup down on a tree stump and held his hands out towards the fire.

He scanned his surroundings, and took careful notice of the staff. Most staff were still zombies, although there were considerably less than there had been in the trees. Some people were taking photos with the staff now, who always managed to stay in character while the pictures were taken. Other people tried to stay as far away from the actors as possible, but this only worked against them. The actors, like true horror-film villains, seemed to smell people's fear and follow them around.

Whilst this was amusing, Jackson also made sure he was alert and checking that none of the staff were acting suspiciously; quite a difficult task given the nature of their job. However, he made sure there was no non-consensual physical contact between the actors and visitors, as well as ensuring none of these 'chases' went too close to the trees.

While he was examining people close to him, a bright, white coat caught his attention. It was worn by a girl who he guessed was nearly twenty. He shuffled closer to her slightly.

"Thanks," She smiled up at a blond-haired young man who had just handed her a drink.

"Your Mom didn't mind us leaving the party that much then?" The boy said.

"No," She said, sipping her drink, which didn't appear to be alcoholic; *college students?,* Jackson thought, "You saw her when we left: happy enough gossiping with everyone."

Jackson switched his gaze back to the blond-haired boy, and saw that he didn't appear to be drinking alcohol either.

The girl had blonde hair herself – much lighter than that of the boy who Jackson assumed was her boyfriend. He couldn't make out every detail of her face, but with the bonfire in front of them blazing wildly, he could see her big, beautiful, green eyes which seemed to shine brighter than the moon of that night.

"What are we going to do first then?" Another young man, this one handing a drink to another girl, asked.

"Try out a maze and then use the fairground to calm ourselves if we have to?" The girl he had just handed a drink to laughed.

"I'm sure it won't be *that* bad," The blonde-haired girl spoke, sounding quite worried and as though she was trying to convince herself.

"It will be fine, babe." Her boyfriend spoke, putting his arm around her.

When Jackson reflected upon that moment afterwards, he realised it was when the feelings of jealousy suddenly began to strangle him, that he felt something more than lust for her.

*

Lincoln walked from inside the large white tent and towards the raging bonfire with his group of friends. Only a couple of them were old enough to buy alcohol at the moment, so they had gone inside to buy drinks while a couple of others waited near the bonfire for them to bring the drinks back.

The group gathered around a fat tree stump, on which they put down all their drinks as they tried to warm themselves up using the bonfire.

As Lincoln stood with his friends, he allowed his gaze to drift towards the horror mazes at the far end of the clearing. They were all lined up against one another. He was excited by all of them, but the one he was most excited about was the 'Bunny-Man Bridge'. It was that specific horror maze which had enabled him to discover the existence of the tour.

Every Halloween there was always news surrounding the local urban legend; sightings reported in the paper or even just a page looking back at the history with some 'expert' discussing where the legend came from and why it was still so prevalent today.

So, October had arrived and everyday Lincoln used the internet to search for news articles relating to the 'Bunny-Man'. One day, he came across an article that was reviewing a new horror tour in Southumberland (a group of reporters from a local paper had been given exclusive access to the event a week before it began so they could advertise it in their paper). As soon as he had read about it, he knew he *had* to go.

Of course, he couldn't let on to his friends how excited he was about the event. He'd had to suggest it as though it was just a place where they could hang out before they went back to college.

Then, last week, after the first night of the tour was the news of the murders in Wald Forest. Lincoln had been instantly drawn in; but the news offered very little detail about the case, as it would until the killer was found and sentenced. Only after all that would the books and documentaries start to be released. *IF* they ever found the killer.

As Lincoln was examining the entrances of the horror mazes and wondering in which order he would like to go through them, a white figure across the bonfire caught his eye. He looked, thinking that it was another actor employed by the event, dressed up as a ghost or maniac doctor. However, his eyes rested upon a beautiful, blonde-haired girl.

She looked about his age, and she was so good-looking that he assumed she must have been one of the 'cool girls' in school and even now in college. If she was, he could have gone over to her and would easily get her. That was an ability that had come with his 'transformation' towards the end of school. It appeared that his suspicions about her were confirmed when he saw the boy that she was with. Lincoln could tell when someone was sporty like him, and this blond guy looked the type and fitted the criteria.

However, Lincoln saw the way that they were acting around one another, and decided that it was best left alone. He didn't want to get into a fight by trying to tempt her away from her boyfriend and ruin the whole night.

She was beautiful though… He tried to place her face. Had she gone to his school? Had he seen her at college? No. Was she even local, or had she travelled here just to visit the Halloween tour?

Lincoln met eyes with her boyfriend and quickly looked away, not wanting to ruin the night that he had been looking forward to so much.

But even then, he continued to steal as many glimpses of her as he could, imprinting every little detail of her into his memory.

As he did so, he couldn't help but feel that they were going to meet again.

*

He walked past the queue to the 'Ghost Train' maze; the line of people looking up at him in horror. He occasionally turned to look at some of them, and was usually met by a frightened pair of eyes which would quickly turn away.

Later that night, he was intending to ensure several pairs of eyes would be looking at him in genuine fear; the kind of fear that was not artificial, but fear that was spawned from desperation.

"He's *tall*." A whisper he had become very used to – not just over the course of the horror tour, but almost his entire life.

As he walked, he scanned. His eyes darted from group to group, person to person, searching for the perfect victims.

Parents with children… He wasn't *that* sick. They were instantly ruled out.

Plenty of teenagers, just like last time; an age which he had not long departed from himself, which he thought was probably why he preferred them so much.

His Mother had probably been around that age too when he was a baby, from the little he could remember of her.

The crowd seemed bigger than last time, which was to be expected with the event being held in a city as populous as Tornwich, but it seemed the murders earlier that month hadn't had a drastic effect on the number of visitors. He thought that was strange given everything he had been reading on the news and social media; given the fear he had sensed among the local population.

Most probably aren't local, he thought.

He stopped walking and looked around.

He looked towards the large bonfire and slowly examined the people gathered around it. He began walking towards it, taking his time and making sure that he looked at every face and judged every person.

His gaze settled upon a pretty girl who seemed to be a year or two away from twenty. She was wearing a puffy, white coat. He suddenly found himself wanting to stroke her blonde hair. He took a step closer towards her, but stopped when he saw that an arm was around her shoulders.

He followed the arm to see what person it was attached to. Her boyfriend, it seemed.

He was pleasantly surprised to find that not only was her boyfriend blond-haired like her, but he was just as pretty as her.

Perfect, he thought.

*

Jackson knew he had to keep an eye on the groups of teenagers. He only had one set of murders to go on, but from his cases in the past he knew killers usually stuck to a certain type of victim. This murderer hadn't slain enough people yet to be classed as a serial killer, but it had all the indications that it was one just beginning their reign of terror.

Jackson was determined to make sure that whoever it was, they would never get the satisfaction of being awarded the title 'serial killer'; most murderers he had encountered saw it as something to be proud of.

Jackson looked at the girl with the white coat on. She seemed safe and secure with her group of friends, he couldn't spend the entire night watching her. So, to avoid her becoming a distraction, he turned and walked away from the bonfire. He'd left his beer there, but didn't think he could hold it any longer anyway, it was just too cold.

He shoved his hands inside the pockets of his hoodie as he walked away.

Jackson had no idea and no plan as to how he was going to catch the killer, he just had to hope something gave them away. He knew that he'd probably have to catch them in the act if he was to have any way of gathering reliable evidence and testimony for an arrest and court case. That's why he had to stay alert and keep an eye on as many groups of teenagers as possible. Thankfully, the clearing was mostly empty space. However, he wouldn't be able to watch the insides of the horror mazes all night, which he thought would be the prime places for someone to snatch a person away.

Jackson, perhaps paying too much attention to his surroundings than directly in front of him, almost walked straight into a member of staff. He managed to notice them out of the corner of his eye at the last second and swerve out of their way.

Turning back, he apologised. The tall clown simply turned his head, almost like an owl, and stared at Jackson before turning back around.

Jackson, rather than turning around and continuing his walk towards the horror mazes, continued to look at the clown.

His hair was black, although there were green patches and little green specks sprinkled throughout, as though some sort of powder had been rubbed through it. From what Jackson had seen of his face, it was white, black around the eyes, red around the lips and on the tip of the nose. For a clown, his costume was fairly ordinary; black trousers and a white shirt. His sleeves were rolled up and revealed pale skin that wasn't painted white. However, he was wearing dark red shoes and pinstriped (yellow and red) suspenders as well as a bow tie of the same colours. He also wore gloves that were bright purple.

You're reading too much into things now, Jackson tried to tell himself, but he watched the young clown, and saw that he was stalking the groups of people seated around the bonfire.

Jackson walked forward and stood next to the clown. He turned and looked up at him but the clown paid no attention; just continued staring at the groups of people around the bonfire.

"You're not cold?" Jackson finally thought of something to say.

The clown turned to him, and for a moment Jackson thought he would stay in character and not answer, just stay sinisterly silent and look away again. The clown shrugged, and did look away, but said: "It's quite nice, actually. It gets warm in there." The clown gestured towards the horror mazes, "So coming out here… Feels like you can breathe again."

Jackson nodded, "Which one do you work in?"

"The 'Ghost Train'."

"You get breaks?"

"There's so many of us in there, they don't notice if you slip away for a few minutes for a quick break. Thankfully, I don't have a big role, so I can do this."

"Well, I won't say anything." Jackson said. To his surprise, the clown seemed like a fairly normal young man.

"Appreciate it."

Jackson took out his badge and ID and showed it to the young, tall clown as he had done to the member of staff at the booths earlier, "I'm part of security tonight. I'll be around here all night, let me know if I'm needed anywhere."

The clown stared at Jackson's ID for longer than Jackson was used to people doing; they usually just glanced at it before struggling for what to say next out of nervousness. After a few moments, Jackson put it back in his pocket, forcing the young man to look back at him.

"Will do, sir." The clown nodded, and then turned back to the bonfire, "We didn't get any trouble last time, but I understand the police's concern with people feeling a bit worried."

Jackson nodded, patted the clown on the back, and turned to walk away, "Hope the night's an easy one for you."

"You too." The clown said.

*

He turned around to make sure that the bald-headed, bearded man was far enough away. He took out his phone, dialled, and put it up to his ear. He held it at a slight distance, not wanting his makeup or the green face paint in his sideburns to smudge against the screen.

His call was answered, but there was no greeting.

"Hello, Father." He said.

"I know you have business to attend to tonight, so let's make this quick." Said Deputy Chief Constable Ralph Cox of the Southumberland Constabulary.

*

"Detective Sergeant James Jackson." He heard his son say.

He didn't fully understand at first, and simply stayed silent for a few moments, before realising that Jackson had defied him and gone to the Halloween tour.

"There shouldn't be any police or security there, I made sure of it."

"Well, he's here."

Cox reclined in his chair and rubbed his eyelids with his free hand, "Have you killed him?"

"Should I?"

Cox lowered his hand and started biting his nails. He would love his son to eliminate Jackson for him, but also knew how much grief it would cause him.

"Raaaaaaalph?"

"I'm your Father, so address me by that title, I think I deserve it after all I've done for you." Cox realised he had leaned forward in his anger and was almost shouting, so reclined again to try and calm himself.

"I will call you whatever I like; you've earned nothing from me."

"I've made sure you were taken care of all your life, I mean... I may not have been there but-"

"You killed my Mother."

"Your Mother was a slut!"

Silence.

"Kill him." Cox finally said. "Bury the body, though. I don't care what you do with the others." Cox knew that there would be more victims than just Jackson that night, but he would be able to cover for his son when it came to those murders. Jackson's murder would be another story, the body had to disappear, or Cox would be under a lot of pressure and that would put everything he'd worked towards in jeopardy.

"Thanks. *Father*."

*

Chloe edged forward slightly. Her eyes darted from side to side, trying to see whatever they could through the darkness. She felt as though she wanted to laugh to try and ease her nervousness, but also as though she wanted to cry out of fear.

She reached out in the darkness to try and find Connor's hand. First, her hand touched his arm, and he seemed to recoil. She whispered his name and his arm came back into reach, and then she slid her hand down his arm until it reached his hand. He gripped her hand in his, and she deduced that he must have been just as scared as she was.

The night air was still bitingly cold. Even with her puffy, white coat on, Chloe still felt as though the air was slicing away at her skin. Like ice-cold blades cutting through the flesh, sending the cold sensation further and further into the body.

Chloe looked to the left and, squinting, could just about see two figures against the dark night sky. It seemed Sarah and Josh were holding onto one another as well.

Everything was silent. Not even the wind shaking the leaves on the trees could be heard. No creatures of the night. Nothing.

Suddenly, there was a loud *click*!

A second later, this was followed by a blinding light turning on to the left of them all – Chloe quickly glanced and saw that it was a large lamp taped to one of the trees on the side of the path they were walking on.

"Help!"

In front of them, crawling towards them along the path, was a woman. Her body was twisted and struggling to pull itself forward. Behind her were lines of blood where she had pulled herself along the path. Her clothes were torn and her skin was red in places – red with blood. It was as though she'd been put through a barbaric amount of torture.

"Help me!" She shouted, and held a hand out towards them in desperation.

Then, from behind her, out of the trees, came the Bunny-Man.

He held his arms out wide, and in one of his hands was his trademark axe, pointing towards the moon, glimmering with joy as it readied to take another victim.

Chloe's first thought was that his costume looked warm, which made her realise just how cold she was; her first instinct wasn't to run in fear or cry out in horror, but to long after the dull pink costume of the Bunny-Man.

The costume looked like something a children's entertainer should be wearing. It was fluffy and pink and the face contained bulging, joyful eyes and a wide, beaming grin. However, the costume was ripped in places, as though victims had struggled against him; but the blood that was splashed across the material was an indication that none of these struggles had succeeded.

The large, costumed maniac stomped forward, and its victim looked back at it and screamed.

Bang!

Smoke flew across the air like a fast-moving fog. The Bunny-Man flew backwards and landed on the floor, dropping his axe.

Chloe's head snapped to the right, and standing between two large trees was a policeman, shakily gripping a gun with two hands.

He lowered his weapon and ran forward towards the injured woman.

"Are you okay?" He asked as he started checking her.

Chloe met eyes with Sarah, who appeared to be more amused than frightened judging by her smile and cocked eyebrow.

"No! Look!"

Chloe looked back to the path, and saw that the Bunny-Man had risen. He was sitting up and wildly searching for his axe. When a furry paw rested upon it, the policeman stood and faced towards Chloe and her group.

"Into the trees!" He cried, and pointed to the part of the forest which he had appeared from, "Follow the rabbits." With that, he turned back around and pointed his gun towards the Bunny-Man, who was now beginning to stand up. The woman on the floor screamed in horror again, and the policeman shouted several warnings.

Connor pulled Chloe's hand and the four of them entered the trees. Almost as soon as they did, several more gunshots rang out.

"Where the fuck do we go?" Chloe asked.

"Follow the rabbits." Sarah calmly replied.

"Above you." Josh followed up with, also sounding calm but with some urgency in his voice.

Chloe looked up and saw dozens of bunny rabbits hanging from tree branches by thick rope. They weren't real and quite obviously teddies, which is why they had probably been placed above head level so that people wouldn't find them too comical.

They started walking forward through the trees, and Chloe would look up every few seconds to make sure that they were on the right path.

"Quickly!" Shouted a voice from behind them, and Chloe recognised it as the policeman's, "He's coming!"

"Oh, shit!" Josh shouted, suddenly sounding scared and not calm at all.

Chloe turned around quickly and saw the policeman following them, almost jogging. Behind him, further in the distance, was a pink figure in hot pursuit and rapidly gaining.

She must have slowed down after turning around, because she felt Connor tug on her hand.

Turning back, looking over Connor's shoulder, she saw what she assumed was the back of the replicated Bunny-Man Bridge, and there was a black, door-shaped cut-out which she guessed was the exit they were meant to go through.

Once through it, it was pitch black.

"Where are we meant to go now?" Chloe asked.

"Forwards!" She heard the policeman shout, "Keep going!" But then his shouts were replaced by screams as the Bunny-Man seemingly caught him.

Connor led them forwards, and they pushed through a plastic, black sheet and came back out into the clearing.

Off to the right of them was the queue to go into the Bunny-Man Bridge horror maze, and it seemed all of the people waiting were looking at them to try and judge how scary an experience they were in for.

"That was fun." Sarah commented and laughed.

"Yeah." Josh nodded, "If you say so."

Chloe turned to Connor, "Never expected it to scare you so much."

"Oh, shut up." He smiled.

They all shared a nervous laugh – even Sarah, so Chloe assumed the last part of the maze, where they were all stuck in the darkness of the bridge, had finally managed to scare her.

They had all already been in the 'Haunted House' maze, which was more like watching a short show at the theatre that you had to move around to watch. It was a story about a ghost that haunted the families that lived there, told by a 'guide' who took them through the house. The ghost was introduced quickly, and it followed – or stalked – the group around the house as they went through, watching them but never saying anything as the story of what happened there unfolded. Actors in each room played out a story from the past that either revealed more about the ghost's life and how it died, or re-enacted the ghost's hauntings. In the last room, the ghost suddenly became more of a poltergeist as the worst of its troubled past was revealed and it started throwing any object it could get its hands on around the room. It ended with the guide hurrying them all out of the house and screaming as the door slammed shut, as though the ghost had caught him before he could escape; rather like the ending to the Bunny-Man Bridge maze. The 'Haunted House' maze had been only mildly scary, and so Chloe felt comfortable carrying on with the rest of the night, convinced that it wouldn't have any impact on her condition.

"Where to next then, gang?" Sarah asked.

"Well, there's only one left." Josh replied.

They all started to make their way over to the 'Ghost Train'.

"Then we can finally go to the fairground afterwards." Sarah said.

Chloe held Connor's hand and leaned her head against his shoulder as they walked, "Are you staying at mine tonight?" She asked.

"Can do." He smiled at her.

She wanted to tell him, she was ready to tell him.

At first she had been scared and in a panic, but now she was excited about it.

They had only been together for a year, but it felt much longer than that because of the way they had bonded straight away and got together so quickly.

They had rarely argued, and when they did it was only over minor issues. Even then, there were never raised voices, just discussions or long silences before they resolved the situation.

Having a baby wouldn't be easy with her and Connor both wanting to go to university next year, but with them both having applied to the University of Tornwich, she felt it would be manageable and her parents and large family would surely be extremely supportive.

She was ready.

But first, the Ghost Train.

*

There had to be something specific he could look for. So far he had just been lingering around, waiting for any sign or indication that there was a killer among them. It wasn't the best tactic, but what else did he have to work with? ... But he *did* have something. He almost felt the lightbulb appear above his head, illuminating his face as he felt his muscles relax, his features soften in light of his new idea.

'The New Bunny-Man?' The newspapers thought it could be a copycat (as much of a copycat killer as you could be when the original never existed, anyway), and he had considered the idea, too.

Perhaps the answer had been so obviously hiding in plain sight that he'd looked past it. He turned around and looked at 'The Bunny-Man Bridge' replica that was serving as one of the three horror mazes that night.

Jackson still didn't want to actually go inside one of the mazes. Not yet anyway. He decided he would stay in the clearing and watch as the people went in and came out. Although he hadn't been watching the horror mazes intently so far that night, he estimated that each group spent a little under or over ten minutes inside each one.

He moved closer to the entrance to the maze, and moved to an angle at which he could see who was going in. A group was just being guided into the darkness of the tunnel, and he managed to get a glimpse of them – a family, two parents and two teenage siblings, it appeared. He watched them go inside and then waited.

He moved to the edge of the clearing so that he could lean against a tree while he kept his gaze fixed on the exit of the maze. By the time the family came out again, he thought it had been a lot longer than ten minutes, but checking his phone saw that it had actually only been seven. They were all there, parents and children, looking panicked and fearful but also amused at the same time.

Jackson watched next group go in and come out, and then the one after that.

He sighed and turned away from the maze. His head was hurting. He leaned back against the tree, this time staring into the blackness of the forest instead of across the clearing.

Jackson let his eyes adjust to the darkness contained inside the forest trees, which were a maze themselves. He worked his eyes slowly across the scene in front of him. Brown tree trunks. Green leaves and sometimes a green bush. The dark, almost black, night sky. The silver stars shining down through the trees and the leaves. A pink humanoid figure.

Jackson felt himself stop breathing. He looked around himself and saw that everyone was carrying on with their night as normal. He turned back to the trees and looked inside again, squinting to try and locate the pink he had just seen against all the darkness of the forest.

Just as he was mentally cursing himself for looking away, his eyes locked onto the figure again. It didn't seem to be moving, was it even a person? It had to be. Was it the Bunny-Man? It was highly likely – and if it was, why wasn't he where he should be, inside the horror maze?

Jackson panicked and felt as though his heart had stopped when he saw the pink figure move. Not only had it moved, but it was getting bigger – it was coming towards him. As it got closer, Jackson saw that this was, in fact, a giant, human bunny, and it was carrying something in its hand. A long, brown object, on the end of which was…

Jackson looked up from the axe and into the eyes of the pink bunny costume as the figure came closer and closer. Jackson reached inside his hoodie and for his harness, and moved his hand along it until he felt his fingers rest upon the handcuffs.

When the figure was only a few metres away, it stopped and dropped the axe before quickly removing the giant bunny head from the rest of the costume.

"You didn't see me here, okay? Please?" The mouth spoke.

Jackson began to think he'd caught his man; someone so desperate not to be seen had to be up to something… but this person was so young, the face of a boy who was still in high school. His voice was desperate, like a child not wanting to be told off, not a killer who didn't want to be caught.

Jackson let his hand drop from the handcuffs and nodded, beginning to understand the situation, "You're not the only one who takes a break, mate, don't worry."

"We all do," The boy cradled the bunny head under his arm and picked the axe back up from the floor, which Jackson now saw was plastic, "But if the bosses found out…" The boy rolled his eyes. "I got to get back to work. Thanks, man!"

"No problem." Jackson mumbled, and turned around again.

He tutted and shook his head at himself.

You're getting too paranoid now.

How long before you arrest someone who's completely innocent just because they give you a small scare?

Nothing was happening.

Maybe he was wrong.

He'd become so convinced by his own theory that he'd started treating it as though it was fact.

Almost half a mile away, he thought; the bodies had been found almost half a mile away from where the tour had been held last time.

Surely that was too far for one man to drag three bodies?

He was beginning to doubt himself. Maybe Cox wasn't being racist or protecting anyone, he was just right in what he had said; he was more experienced than Jackson and knew that this 'lead' would in fact lead to nothing.

Jackson, giving up on keeping an eye on the clearing, ventured into the trees behind the three horror mazes. If nothing was going to happen at the event, then he would search the trees for anything suspicious as he had earlier that afternoon.

He would search half a mile in every single direction if he had to.

*

Five in one night.

The two couples and now the detective.

FIVE.

Well, he had his axe now, at least. He'd rushed back to the tents and got it after his phone call.

He was ready.

Five.

No problem, he thought, *no problem at all*, and started following the detective into the trees.

*

Jackson just kept walking straight ahead.

There had to be something, he had to be right.

His career was on the line now, and he knew that his life probably was too – that was the price people paid for being in Cox's way.

Unexpectedly, Jackson stepped into a small clearing.

He stopped and looked around. Opposite him was a blue tent. To the left of him was a blue tent. To the right of him was a blue tent.

"What?..." He breathed, and his heart suddenly starting thudding against his chest.

He quickly reached into his pocket and took out his phone, turning the camera-torch on. He could see more clearly now, but there was nothing extra to see.

It's nothing, he told himself, *just people camping.*

"Detective Jackson?"

He lowered his torch and turned around.

The clown member of staff from earlier. Jackson had probably stumbled upon a staff area, and was probably about to be told he had to leave.

But wait...

"I didn't tell you my name..." Jackson said.

"It was on your card." The clown replied.

"Oh." Jackson nodded, "Of course."

That's why he'd looked at it for so long.

Jackson suddenly saw something glimmer in the light of his torch, and realised with mounting horror, that the clown was carrying an axe. A real axe.

"What's your name?" Jackson asked.

"Cox." The clown said, and walked forward.

"I see." Jackson said, and suddenly everything made sense, "I don't want this to have to be a struggle."

"A pity." Said the clown, "I do."

Then, with speed too fast for Jackson to react, the clown suddenly raised his axe into the air and brought it crashing into Jackson's knee.

Pain shot through Jackson's leg and he collapsed to the floor.

He opened his eyes and quickly looked down, expecting to see that he had only half a leg left, or part of it hanging off.

However, he'd clearly been hit with the blunt end of the axe; his leg was still intact.

Now that he knew he was able, he tried to make his way back to his feet, but was flattened to the cold forest floor by a foot smashing into the back of his neck.

"I spoke to my Father earlier." The clown stated, "Do you know what he said?"

"Fuck… you." Jackson managed to spit against the leaves and the mud.

"No. That would inappropriate of him to say, don't you think?" The clown laughed.

Jackson looked up at him, and it seemed he was as tall as the trees that surrounded them; his head up in the sky with the treetops.

"He gave me permission to kill you."

Cox the clown looked up, "Come here." He demanded.

Jackson tried to look at who he was talking to, but couldn't move his head from its current position.

"Will you keep an eye on this one if I go back to the 'Ghost Train' and fetch the others?"

"Yes, boss." Came the obedient reply, as a short, chubby figure – much the opposite to Cox the clown – stepped into view. "Hello!" He waved at Jackson. His face was painted white, with black lips, black circles around the eyes and one on the tip of the nose. His face paint matched Cox's, but with black instead of red. His costume also matched Cox's, but again, this short, chubby clown had black shoes, black and white pinstriped suspenders and a black and white bow tie in contrast to the bright colours Cox was wearing.

"Go on, then." Cox said.

The fat clown walked forward and drove his foot into Jackson's face, rendering him unconscious.

*

What if I've missed them? He thought, rushing through the trees and back to the Ghost Train.

There will be other opportunities, he told himself, *follow them, and wait, and then take them. You can do it.*

But already he was fearful. He was desperate; he wanted that lovely girl and her lovely boyfriend. He'd have to take their friends too, otherwise people would be around searching for them all night. He couldn't afford that. The other couple would just be a bonus rather than a burden, he tried to convince himself. It would be a struggle taking four people into the forest all at once, but he was certain he could do it.

He rushed forward, he knew he was nearly there now.

He hoped that he would reach there in time.

*

Chloe was surprised to see that the 'Ghost Train' horror maze did seem very similar to the traditional ghost trains found on fairgrounds. Visitors were being seated in small carts that were then driven into the building electronically. However, when the carts were coming back out, they were empty. Chloe assumed that meant there would be walking again; which made sense considering it was meant to be a 'maze', even though the other two attractions hadn't been much of a maze either.

"I don't want to go back to college." Sarah huffed.

Josh put his arm around her, "None of us do."

"It's not so bad." Chloe said.

Sarah looked at her, and it was as though Chloe could see the fires of rage within her pupils, "We have mock exams on what we've done so far when we go back."

"Oh… I forgot about that… Yeah, I don't want to go back either." Chloe smiled, "I take it nobody's revised?"

A silence fell over the group as they all looked at one another in mutual understanding.

"Nobody has… Probably." Connor said.

"I might do a bit over the weekend." Chloe commented.

"Yeah, probably best to." Josh replied.

Sarah groaned, "I suppose I'll look over my notes."

"We can help each other." Connor nudged Chloe and smiled.

"That sounds distracting."

"Exactly."

"Maybe we can do that, as well." Josh turned to Sarah.

"Why did I take law?" Sarah rolled her eyes.

"Yeah… Not the most erotic of topics." Josh nodded and laughed.

"Not because of that you sex pest." Sarah retorted.

"Funny," Chloe stated, turning to Connor, "I called Connor the same thing earlier."

"So you *did* have a night of frightening passion after all?" Sarah winked at Chloe, "Did you dress up as well?"

"Well, Connor was in his football-"

"That's enough!" Connor quickly declared.

"These men," Sarah began, "Always talk about wanting it, but then don't like us going into details about it."

Chloe and Sarah laughed, and Chloe could just about see Josh and Connor meet eyes, looking very unamused.

"Come on… Sex pests." Sarah laughed, and started walking towards the small cart the four of them were to be seated in. This one was given a horror-circus theme: on the front of it was a clown head that looked demonic with its yellow eyes and sharp teeth.

It was their turn to ride the Ghost Train.

*

Jackson kept his eyes firmly shut. He'd already tried to open them, and it hadn't ended well. Everything was spinning.

"Detective?"

Jackson's mouth and throat felt dry, and no matter how hard he tried to gather enough spit in his mouth to swallow, he couldn't do it.

"Detective?"

He moved his lips to speak, but the sound wouldn't release from his throat; it was trapped. As much as he wanted to open his eyes to show some acknowledgement at being called, he didn't want to throw up.

"DETECTIVE!"

Jackson pushed himself up into a sitting position with his hands. It felt like he was going to fall, and so it took all the strength he had to hold himself up. He tried to push words out again, but nothing would come.

"Here."

He reached a hand out and searched slowly, until his hand bumped against something cold. A bottle. He gripped it, twisted the lid off and pressed it to his lips. He gulped it down until he was sucking the air out of the bottle.

He put it down and slowly opened his eyes.

He was still dizzy, but it was nowhere near as bad as it had been the first time he had opened his eyes.

Jackson realised that he was in a tent. In front of him, blocking the way out, was Cox the clown's 'sidekick' (that's what Jackson deduced from what he had seen). The short, colourless clown barely had to arch his neck to stop his head from touching the top of the tent, whereas Cox would surely struggle to even enter one of the tents without almost crawling.

"Why are you helping him?" Jackson tried, not actually expecting to get answers.

"We grew up together." The black and white clown said.

"That's not a valid reason for being an accomplice to murder, is it?" Jackson said viciously, trying to make the clown fear being arrested and going to court.

"We lived in the same children's home." The clown replied calmly and casually, "We arrived there at the same time, with similar… experiences."

"You're not a Cox as well?"

"Unfortunately not."

"Ralph Cox brings fortune to nobody but himself."

"And his son."

"I thought you said you were both in a children's home?"

"We were."

"I'd hardly call that fortunate."

The clown didn't say anything.

"And now, I'm guessing because of his fucked-up childhood caused by his 'wonderful' Father, your friend likes to kill people. And you, with similar 'experiences', follow him around like his little bitch."

"Be quiet." The clown growled.

"So what is your name?"

"Nice try." The clown grinned.

"If you're so confident I'm going to be killed tonight, what's the harm in telling me your name?"

"You'll die without the satisfaction of knowing." The clown spat, and launched forward.

Jackson tried to stand, but pain suddenly shot through his leg from where Cox the clown had hit him with his axe. He fell backwards despite trying desperately to stay upright, and for the second time that night the short, chubby clown booted him in the face. Jackson wondered, as darkness descended across his vision, if the girl in the puffy white coat was safe.

And then he wondered if that would be his last thought as he slipped into unconsciousness once again.

*

Everything went dark again, and Chloe felt a breeze start to brush past her; they were being taken outside. The interior of the 'Ghost Train' had been what she'd have expected to see on a real fairground ghost train; different scenes of horror characters such as Dracula looming over an unfortunate victim about to have their blood drained. Every now and then, Chloe would also feel a hand brush against the back of her head, and from the groans and screams she sometimes heard from the others, she knew they were being touched as well. She guessed a member of staff must have jumped on the back of their clown-themed cart as soon as they'd entered the building.

The cart moved forward slowly, and Chloe saw black flaps start to lift before the moon and stars appeared above them.

Judging by the tracks, Chloe guessed they were going to be led into the forest again to be chased by more costumed maniacs. However, the cart came to a halt just before it entered the trees. All four of them sat in silence and anticipation.

"Now what?" Sarah asked.

*

He watched them from inside the trees.

He knew the cart was meant to reverse and go back into the 'Ghost Train' building, taking them around more horror scenes before bringing them outside again for the final scare, but he was going to take advantage of the situation; he had a few seconds in which to act.

He ran out of the trees and towards them.

*

"Come!" The tall clown shouted as he rushed towards them, "Into the trees with me!"

Chloe started to climb out of the cart, and met eyes with the clown as she did. When standing, she realised just how tall he was. Connor, the tallest of their group, didn't even come close to reaching the clown's height.

"Quickly! Follow me!" He exclaimed and started walking back towards the trees.

As they entered the trees, Chloe looked back and saw the cart they were seated in reversing back into the building.

That must be why it comes back out empty at the entrance, she thought.

It was very dark inside the trees and away from the lights of the horror tour's various attractions. If it wasn't for the clown's bright coloured suspenders and shoes, she wouldn't know which way to go.

They carried on following the clown, who Chloe thought was not much older than them. She kept expecting horror figures to start jumping out of the trees and scaring them, or the clown to come to a stop and begin telling them a scary tale, before a short scene followed.

But none of those things happened.

They just kept walking.

Sarah turned to Chloe and Connor, "Is anything going to bloody happen?" She whispered.

"You must be quiet." The clown demanded, and Chloe guessed that there was going to be a story about a monster in the trees that they were going to disturb, and it was going to start chasing them as the Bunny-Man had.

The clown finally stopped and stood to one side.

The sound of leaves crunching underneath their feet came to a sudden halt.

"Into the clearing." He pointed.

Chloe clung to Connor as they followed Sarah and Josh. Once in the clearing, Chloe could barely see anything, she stood on her toes and could make out blue shapes. After some moments in which her eyes adjusted to the darkness, she realised they were tents.

As expected, Chloe saw a figure emerge from one of the tents.

"Good evening!" It said happily.

Then, suddenly, Chloe felt Connor ripped from her side and thrown to the floor. Before she had time to react, she felt her shoulders grabbed. She, too, was shoved to the ground.

She saw Josh looking at her in fear. Whoever had emerged from the tent was running towards Sarah and Josh, and Chloe tried to warn them, but no words were able to escape from her tight throat. Instead, all that squeezed through was the slightest of noises, something she was sure could be heard from a mouse.

The figure came to a sudden stop and grunted. From what she could make out, it looked as though the figure had run into Sarah's fist.

"Chloe?"

"I'm here!" She wasn't sure who'd said her name.

She couldn't see Josh anymore, and she hadn't been able to see Connor since he'd been thrown to the floor.

As she looked at Sarah, who was walking towards her, she saw a white circle above her head. It was following her, coming closer and closer.

"Sarah!" Chloe somehow managed to shout.

But it was too late.

Sarah disappeared into the darkness of the forest ground.

Then, all that could be heard was struggling, before Chloe herself was grabbed and dragged. She kicked out with her feet, and tried to strike out with her hands, but whoever was holding her had a strong grip that wasn't weakening. She was lifted and plunged into further darkness and then heard the sound of a zip.

She'd been put in one of the tents.

Holding back tears as she continued to listen to the struggles outside, she whispered Connor's name.

No response.

"Connor?" She spoke, as her voice began to break.

A hand touched her arm.

"I'm here." He said.

She reached out and hugged him, and held him tighter than she ever had before.

Chapter Four

James Jackson clung to his Mother's dress. He didn't really understand what was happening, but knew that it was bad. They were talking about his sister. Something had happened. Something BAD. Had she done something bad herself? Something at college, at work? Or, even worse, had something bad happened to her? That thought made Jackson terrified. Had she been in an accident? She had only been driving for a few months, and he'd been driven around by her before; it was nowhere near as good as his Dad's driving. The worst possibility of all, in Jackson's mind, was the one that screamed loudest in his head; it was echoing inside his skull, paining his small brain: had someone done something bad to her?

"We can drive you to the scene if you'd like?" The police officer said calmly to his shaken Mother.

"Can he stay in the car?" His Mother patted his head.

"Of course."

She didn't even go back into the house to fetch her bag or make sure all the windows and doors were shut, they just left instantly from the doorstep.

They rode in the back of the police car, and not much was said along the way. Jackson continued to hold onto his Mother, and as much as he wanted to ask what had happened, he didn't. One reason was that he didn't think she would tell him, but secondly he wasn't even sure he actually wanted to know himself.

So Jackson just remained silent.

The drive was an uncomfortably long one, and Jackson wondered why his sister had travelled so far. When the car started to approach the lively city centre, he guessed that she must have gone for a day out shopping with her friends. These thoughts were almost immediately confirmed by one of the officers in the front of the car.

"Her car was identified by one of her friends. It's on the car park over there." And he pointed towards the enormous car park in front of the huge shopping complex.

"Okay. Thank you." His Mother replied, her voice steady and emotionless.

Jackson looked at her, and her head was turned towards the window, but she didn't appear to actually be looking at anything. She was just staring.

The drive lasted some minutes longer, until finally the car was parked alongside trees Jackson was vaguely familiar with. As far as he knew, this was Wald Forest.

A few metres down the road, a small part of the forest had clearly been sectioned off. Tape surrounded some of the trees and barriers were erected along the street to make sure people didn't wander too close to the trees to see whatever had happened. There were several police officers on the street and Jackson could also see a few moving around beyond the line of the trees.

Across the street, local residents were on their front gardens, looking across the busy road to try and see what was happening. Some of them had gathered into groups and were pointing and talking, seemingly speculating or relaying what they had heard about what had happened.

"Stay here, JJ." His Mother said and left the car along with the police officers.

Now he was alone.

He looked across the street again and saw that most people had stopped talking and were now just watching. He looked at his Mother who was being led into the trees, underneath the tape, by some police officers.

They weren't going to tell him what had happened. As much as he didn't want to know, he knew he had to find out, or he'd never be given the full story.

No police officers were close to the car anymore, and so he judged that now was the best time to start moving.

He climbed across the back seat and opened the door. He opened it slightly and lowered himself from the backseat, moving slowly and quietly, ensuring he didn't draw attention in his direction. When he was out and standing on the street, he gently eased the door back as close to closed as he could without making any unnecessary noise.

Turning around, he quickly ran from the car making for the trees.

Once out of sight under the cover of the trees, he stopped and listened.

It seemed as though he'd gone unnoticed.

He hoped that his sister was just injured, and that's why he and his Mother had been made to come all the way to the forest to see her. However, there didn't seem to be an ambulance nearby preparing to take an injured patient to the hospital. He didn't like that thought and so he cast it from his mind. He'd always mused that it was like putting his fingers in his ears and making NEEE NORRR sounds when he didn't want to hear something and was always inwardly impressed at how successfully he was able to change the focus of his thoughts from where he didn't want them to be.

Jackson knew what was most likely to have happened, but it wasn't a certainty; while there was still hope there was no need to worry, no need to get upset, no need to cry.

He crouched low and moved from tree to tree, trying to get as close to the sectioned-off area as he could.

"How long has she been dead?"

Jackson stopped and clutched onto a tree laying his body flat against the cover of the thick trunk.

"Few hours by the looks of it."

His sister had gone out that morning, before Jackson had woken. He hadn't thought to ask where she'd gone; he'd just assumed she'd gone out with her friends, which was what she usually did at the weekend.

"Is that the Mother who just walked past?"

"Think so. The friends told us where she lived."

"Jesus…"

Jackson started moving again, rushing forward more quickly this time until more tape came into view. He stopped when he saw his Mother. She was looking at the floor.

Jackson crept forward again until he could see the forest floor beneath his Mom.

Leaves. He looked further forward. More leaves.

Further forward again.

He saw her eyes first. Open and looking in his direction, but wide, glazed and lifeless.

He looked away and covered his own eyes with his hands.

Taking a deep breath, he looked back. He couldn't break down now, he'd have to go back the car in a minute.

He didn't look at the floor again, but at his Mother. He could see now that her hands were clutched to her face. A tall police officer was standing across from her, on the other side of the body, his helmet shadowed most of his face, but Jackson could see his mouth moving.

Cox.

Jackson's eyes snapped open.

His sister's murder had been what had driven him to go into the police force. They'd never caught the person who did it, and neither had he despite using all of the resources at his disposal to try and find new leads in the case that was now over twenty years old.

How could he have forgotten that Cox was there?

Racist.

Jackson wondered if Cox even remembered the murder, or if he even knew how it related to Jackson.

Racist.

Probably not.

Bodies in Wald Forest.

Murders...

Jackson took all of it personally.

He sat up, and instantly became dizzy, blood rushing from his head.

He fell backwards again and the torture of slipping in and out of unconsciousness began.

In the moments when he was able to form thoughts, all he could think about was how he knew it would be a while before he could get up and move properly.

Bodies in Wald Forest…

*

During the school holidays a couple of weeks ago, when out in the city centre with his Mom, Lincoln had come across a book. His Mom was in the clothes shop next door, and so Lincoln had gone into a book shop instead. He had become so wrapped up in the book he had discovered that instead of him having to go back into the clothes shop to his Mother as he always did, she ended up coming to find him. How long had he been reading it? The amount of time she always spent in those shops, it must have nearly been an hour.

"Want to buy it?" She'd asked, ripping his attention away from it as she walked up to him.

"Okay," He'd replied, "Please."

As soon as they'd got home he spent all day reading it. 'Britain's Psychos' was the title of the book, and it ran through a brief history of some of the countries' most famous serial killers. It ran in chronological order, and so 'Jack the Ripper' had been the opening section (it was also the largest section, and Lincoln had only just about finished it in the book shop before his Mom came in).

Late that night, Lincoln finally finished the book in bed. One of the final cases that the book looked at was that of Landon Barker, who as it turned out had been a teacher in Tornwich: right here! Throughout the 1980s he'd killed students and fellow members of staff, as well as eating parts of them, hiding the remains in his house, garden and even Wald Forest.

Then, in the 1990s, after being locked up for a few years Barker had escaped and gone on another killing spree. He killed a group of college students who had been camping in Wald Forest. One of them had survived the massacre, and when she had contacted the police after escaping the forest she told them what had happened, detailing how Barker had attacked her, but she'd managed to grab hold of a knife and stab him in the neck. She told police he was dead, that he must have bled out; there was no way he could have survived such a wound.

But since that frightening event, Landon Barker had not been seen or heard from again, he had simply vanished...

After reading that, Lincoln read into the case some more, finding newspaper articles online with the headlines from the original murders and then the second time, after Barker had escaped. Lincoln started to print these off, as well as photos of Barker and his victims, and started to put together a scrapbook of the case. He also made notes around the photos; a small biography of Landon Barker and his victims around the shots of them, and details of the murders around crime scene photos.

Even at school, at lunch times when he wasn't playing football he would make excuses to his friends so that he could sneak off to the IT rooms and conduct more research on the case to add to his notes when he got home. Sometimes, he would also read about other killers to try and get a better understanding of the way their minds worked; something he thought might aid him in working out what was likely to have happened to Landon Barker after he disappeared. Lincoln also became embroiled in trying to work out other mysteries, such as scanning through the Jack the Ripper suspects and familiarising himself with that case for when he moved on from Tornwich's very own cannibal killer.

Lincoln stared at the computer screen, reading a newspaper article about Landon Barker that he'd somehow missed. It wasn't about anything new that Barker had done, but was a local reporter writing about the similarities between Barker and a cannibal killer in a film that had been released that year – 1991. The reporter had also got the chance to meet with Barker and interview him, and wrote about his experience.

As Lincoln read through the article he felt a hand tap his shoulder, snapping him out of the trance he always entered when doing his research.

He turned, not thinking to close the article, believing it didn't matter.

"What you reading?" The boy who had questioned him was someone who played football regularly, as he did, but who'd never really spoken to him much before beyond the limited conversations that take place in the middle of a match.

Lincoln looked back to the computer screen and then again at the boy. "Just... Erm... It's about a-"

"'Teacher who killed and ate several of his co-workers, as well as the students he taught.'" The boy read from the computer screen.

Lincoln nodded. He'd never spoken to anyone about it before beyond his parents, so didn't know what reaction to expect. Was this boy about to take interest in it as he had?

"What the fuck is wrong with you, man?"

No, was the clear answer.

"It's just-" But Lincoln didn't have time to defend his interest, the boy turned and walked out of the IT room.

Lincoln sighed and logged out of the computer. He would go and play football instead, then. School was clearly a place he could no longer do research.

When he reached the pitch, the reaction of everyone hit him like a punch in the face. He walked onto the field and set his bag down, and realised that most people were staring at him.

His heart felt as though it had lurched into his throat; what was going on?

He stood there for a few moments, not knowing what to do, before the boy who had seen him reading the article in the IT room started whispering to one of the other boys. However, his stage whispers obviously intentionally loud enough for Lincoln to hear.

"Careful," He smirked, "He might eat you." Then, he laughed a little.

Another boy, standing near the goal, suddenly ran forward towards the two boys. His arm was held up high in the air, holding an imaginary knife. When he reached them, he started bringing his arm repeatedly down on them, making screeching noises with each imaginary stab like the music from a horror film as brutal, masked murderer claimed another helpless victim.

Most of the boys were laughing now, and all of them started acting out similar scenes of murder or making jokes about Lincoln being a killer.

News always spread so fast around school, so Lincoln should have seen this coming. He picked up his bag and quickly walked away from the football pitch, still hearing the laughter from the boys as they continued to mock him…

Lincoln wiped sweat from his head. His hand was shaking slightly.

He didn't play football again, after that. Not at school, at least. In fact, not many people were friends with him after that day. The comments and laughter continued for weeks afterwards, eventually dying down after a few months when they got a little bored of repeating the same lines; but even in the last year of school, people still occasionally made fun of his interest, using him when they ran out of other people to pick on.

After that day, when they had all laughed at him, he'd gone home to an empty house. He always had a couple of hours alone until his parents finished work. He'd gone through the entire house, searching for something. Eventually, when he was in the shed in the back garden, he found what he was looking for.

Weights. His parents had gone through a fitness phase a while ago, but had very quickly got tired of it. So Lincoln took the weights up to his bedroom and had started to use them. He had to change his image if he was going to stop the people at school mocking him.

He hadn't been the shortest person, but he was definitely one of the skinniest back in his school days. That had needed to change, and so he changed it…

"Lincoln. Are you okay?"

He looked over at his group of friends and realised how much he was sweating. He tried to laugh it off, "Yeah, it's that fucking fire." He unzipped his jacket and took it off, "Too fucking hot."

"It's all that muscle." One of the girls said and walked over to him, putting her hand around the top of his arm and squeezing.

Lincoln smiled. *Phew!*

One of the boys rolled their eyes, "Don't. You'll make him think he's special again."

"But I am special." Lincoln smiled, and flexed his arm. "See?"

"Oh!" The girl with her hand on it exclaimed.

Everything was normal, everything was fine, they didn't suspect a thing...

*

Chloe, absentmindedly, started running her hand through Connor's hair, sweeping it backwards and styling it for him as best as she could. His hair was short on the sides and back, but there was enough on the top to mess with. She parted it on the left and started pushing the rest of it to the right. She examined the colours; she always found it so fascinating. His hair was blond, but different shades. Some strands were almost brown, whilst others were the same shade as her own hair.

"Are you enjoying yourself?" Connor asked.

"Leave him alone, for God's sake." Sarah demanded.

Chloe looked at her, "You're one to talk." Sarah was holding onto Josh's arm and resting her head on his shoulder, but sat up straight and let go of him after Chloe's comment.

"It's for warmth. Nothing else." Sarah said.

"Thanks." Josh rolled his eyes.

Chloe turned back to Connor, ran a hand through his hair once more to make it as neat as possible, and then leaned back. "Perfect," She smiled, "You look pretty now."

"Great." Connor sighed sarcastically, but then smiled at her to show he was just teasing.

"We better go to tutorial." Chloe said, and began gathering her things and putting them in her bag from off the café table.

"And we need to go to law." Sarah tapped Josh's arm and stood, almost mirroring Chloe's actions.

Once ready, they all walked out of the college café together and towards the classrooms. They parted when Sarah and Josh reached the stairs they needed to use to reach their class, and that left Chloe and Connor alone as they headed towards their classroom.

"We going to mine afterwards?" Chloe asked.

"It is Tuesday, isn't it?" Connor replied.

"I just like to make sure. You might have other plans."

"Never on a Tuesday, that's our afternoon together."

Both of them finished at the same time on a Tuesday; after their tutorial class, which usually ran for no more than half an hour, most times even less. And since they had just finished lunch, it meant they had many hours in the afternoon to spend together when they'd usually be in lessons. Their free periods should be for revision, as they were repeatedly told by teachers, but nobody really listened to that...not until it came to exam season, anyway.

Chloe and Connor sat next to one another as always; in the same places they'd sat a year ago when they'd first met and sat in silence with the rest of the class as the teacher began running through the usual university applications preparation presentations that dominated this lesson every week. It was still early, and so the teacher wasn't being forceful and pushy about their applications yet, but simply kept warning them that they had to start thinking about where they wanted to go, what they wanted to study and what they were going to write to the university in their applications.

Chloe and Connor had already talked about where they wanted to go; the University of Tornwich. Chloe wanted to continue studying English, whilst Connor was deliberating about whether to take a business or media course, or perhaps do a joint degree. Both of them had also said they didn't want to apply for anywhere else, so they were taking a bit of a risk, but felt confident they would attain the necessary grades.

After fifteen minutes, they were given permission to leave.

Chloe and Connor rushed to the college exit and towards the car park, where they got into his car and he started driving them towards her house.

"Have you decided what to study yet?" Chloe asked as the car turned onto the road from the car park.

"I've still just been reading over the course outlines on the website. I'm just going to apply for all three possibilities I think. I'm definitely going to Tornwich Uni anyway, so that will give me a chance to decide later on if I need to."

"Sounds like a good idea." Chloe nodded.

"Are you just applying for literature?" Connor returned her interest in their future education.

"I think so. Language is just... boring. Interesting at times, but boring. Creative writing is a possibility, but from what I've read that sounds like it's part of the literature course anyway; there are some modules especially for it."

"Go for it then." Connor looked at her briefly and smiled before turning his attention back to the road.

Usually, when they got inside her house, it was Connor who started suggestively tugging at her clothes and kissing her before she gave in and they went to her bedroom. Today, though, it was her. As soon as they walked through the front door she forced his shirt off before he did the same to her, and then they went to her bedroom.

That, as far as Chloe could work out, was when they'd made the baby.

As she held onto him inside the tent, the memory of that day was what came back to her. They had spent time with their friends, talked about the future, and made a new life. They were still young; years away from twenty, but thinking about all of that made Chloe feel like an old woman who was ready to settle down.

She almost laughed, despite the situation she was in.

Then, she almost cried, believing it was unlikely any of those things would ever happen again or be finished.

"I'm pregnant." She whispered.

Connor didn't react.

Had she said it too quietly?

"We need to try and escape." He said.

"Connor." She said, quietly but firmly.

He pushed back slightly and looked at her.

"I'm pregnant." She repeated.

For a moment, she could just about see the way his eyes lit up and his lips curled into a smile.

But then the tent was unzipped, and a small, fat clown entered.

He zipped up the tent again, and they were plunged into darkness once more.

*

He hid under his blanket.

He used his pillow to try and cover his ears.

None of it worked; he could still hear them.

"I know you've still been working!" He shouted, "Why?! I give you everything you need!"

"No, Ralph, you give me everything you want me to have!"

Crack!

"You're a control freak!" She screamed.

"I just wanted to help you." He said, more calmly this time.

"You did. But now…"

"I took you out of that way of life. I didn't want you to be arrested and go to prison for it. Isn't it better now? But you can't seem to let go, it's as though you like it! Have you done it while our son is in the house?! Tell me you haven't."

Silence.

"You fucking bitch."

"I need the money, Ralph."

"You need the sex more like!"

Crack!

He threw the blanket off and climbed out of the bed.

There were sounds of a struggle, before his Mother managed to screech: "I'll go to the papers!" Then everything fell silent again.

He moved slowly across the hallway and towards their bedroom.

"That's right. How would they feel about this? What would happen to all your plans and your schemes then you sick bastard?"

"It would probably help my image." He replied after some seconds of silence, "There will be split opinion, I'm sure, but the times are changing. They'll say how I led us into a new era; women like you aren't thrown into prison but helped instead."

"You're delusional."

"Go on, then. DO IT." He tried, "I'll just spin it to help me. I'll probably just land another promotion from it." He chuckled.

"What about the girl?"

"What girl?"

"The one they found in the forest the other week."

"What about her?"

"It was a hate crime, wasn't it?"

"We're looking into it."

"You know who did it."

His Father didn't say anything.

"You're covering for them."

"Why would I do that?" He replied, as though it was a ridiculous accusation.

"Because you agree with them! You want them to kill more of 'their kind'!"

Crack!

"Don't be so stupid!"

He shoved their door open slightly. His Mother was holding her cheek, his Father was looking at her, they were quite close to one another.

"I knew your views Ralph but I never thought you'd go this far… She was a girl! Imagine if you were found out and someone killed our son to get back at you!"

"There's a good, simple way to avoid that."

"How?"

"Don't go to the fucking papers!"

"Scared now?" His Mother smiled, "Yeah, I'll go to the papers. Tell them everything, and then me and your 'son' are out of here."

She started to walk away from him, but he grabbed the back of her long, blonde hair and slammed her down onto the bed.

"You aren't going anywhere." He growled.

He jumped on top of her, holding her down with his body weight, and wrapped his hands around her throat. It seemed they went all the way around; his Mother looked like a tiny, helpless princess in the grip of an angry, villainous giant in one of his books.

He wanted to be her saviour, like the brave knights in those books.

But he couldn't. He was frozen to the spot. His legs wouldn't move.

All he could do was watch as his Father squeezed the life out of his Mother.

That was his earliest memory, and that was where it ended.

His Father probably thought he couldn't remember it, but he'd let him know differently over the phone earlier that night.

"Get off her!"

He turned to one of the tents. Had that been where he'd put the blonde-haired couple? It was.

He quickly walked over towards the tent and unzipped it. He saw the boy grappling with a short, round figure as the girl backed away from them.

Cox reached inside and grabbed his childhood friend by one of his suspenders and dragged him towards him, "Leave her alone."

"Boss! I-"

"Yes, I know exactly what you were doing." Cox looked back inside the tent, surprised the boy hadn't made a move against them and tried to escape. However, he was busy comforting his girlfriend who was sobbing quietly in the corner of the tent.

"Did you touch her?" Cox whispered.

"I tried to! You tell me I can have the women."

"Not this one." Cox growled and pulled him out of the tent, "Have the other one." He permitted, and let go of him. He watched him walk across the small clearing towards the other tent, which he entered and sounds of protest and a struggle quickly filled it.

Cox turned back to the tent he was stood at.

As much as he might want to at times, he couldn't bring himself to touch the women in that way; he had seen the way men had treated his Mother. Not just his Father, but her 'customers' as well.

He tried his best to show some respect for women in that way, he wouldn't ever touch them as his friend did, especially not one who looked so much like his young Mother.

*

"I'm sorry about him." The tall clown apologised as he entered the tent.

"If you're not going to hurt us, why keep us here? Just let us go." Connor turned to him and pleaded.

"Whatever gave you the idea I'm not going to hurt you?" The tall clown smiled, and zipped the tent once again.

Outside, the sounds of a struggle continued, and Chloe heard Sarah scream before almost immediately being silenced. She couldn't hear Josh anymore. The sounds suddenly stopped. There were a few moments were everything was silent and still, and then there was a *click!* Following this, a light suddenly beamed through the tent. Chloe looked at where the light seemed to be coming from, and from the sound that had been made knew that a light on a tree had been turned on – just like in the Bunny-Man Bridge horror maze.

Is this still part of the attraction? Chloe questioned, as though there was still some hope that the situation she and her friends were in couldn't be real.

Everything was still shadowed and dark, but much clearer than it had been.

The sounds of a struggle returned.

Chloe's eyes darted around the tent, looking for any way that she and Connor could get around the tall clown and escape. If he was smaller, Chloe would feel confident that her and Connor's combined strength would be enough to knock him to the floor long enough for them to escape, but he was so tall that she felt they didn't stand a chance. He seemed slim, and not as broad or as muscular as Connor was, but she was sure that he carried a lot of power with his size, and so felt the risk wasn't worth it.

Smack!

The clown had swung something into his hand. Something long that Chloe couldn't quite see in the dark, but as she moved her gaze across the clown's body, she finally saw the glimmering head of an axe in his hand – in the other must have been the end of the handle, which was held horizontally across his body and too dark a shade of brown to be seen (even with the light outside now turned on).

"Move away from each other." The clown demanded calmly.

Chloe reached out to find Connor's hand, and he moved his head close to hers. Just as she thought he was going to whisper something to her, the clown spoke again.

"Move." He repeated, and pointed his axe at them; the shining head dazzling her gaze, blurring her vision so that the white head of the clown looked like a ghostly orb floating around the tent.

Chloe, feeling terror rise up and consume her body, began to shake as Connor did as the clown had commanded and moved to the other side of the tent. Chloe felt some relief as the clown turned away from her, but felt panic-induced vomit begin to rise as he switched his sights towards Connor.

"Turn over."

"What?" Connor breathed.

"Turn. Over." The clown repeated slowly.

Connor obeyed.

"If either of you try anything…" The clown began, and slowly turned his head to look at Chloe, "I'll chop his legs off."

In one moment of desperate hope, Chloe's hand fell upon her pocket. It was empty, her phone was gone. Of course it was, they weren't stupid enough to allow her to keep it. They must have taken everyone else's, too. But when? She couldn't remember. Perhaps they'd done it during the struggle.

Now she felt completely helpless. There was nothing she could do. Nothing at all.

Chloe, to avoid streams of tears rolling down her face like a raging waterfall, squeezed her eyes tightly shut, so tight that it hurt. She listened, and heard Sarah screaming. As bad as it made her feel, and as much as she wanted to help her friend, she had to shut that sound out; right now, she wanted to focus on Connor.

There were sounds of a small struggle, but nothing that sounded like fighting. Chloe heard Connor grunting and the clown sometimes uttering demands like "keep still." Then there was a sound which gave away what was happening; a sound that resembled that final tug as a shoelace was tied, but louder.

She opened her eyes. She had to see.

Squinting, she could see Connor's legs were pressed together, bounded by something she couldn't quite make out.

She became so absorbed in looking at Connor and feeling frightened now that their only hope (however slim) of forcing their way out of the tent was gone that she didn't notice the clown was coming towards her until he grabbed her legs.

She screamed, stopped herself, and wriggled her legs, trying to free them of the madman's grip.

"Stop."

She, like Connor had, obeyed.

Her legs were pushed together and wrapped in something thick and strong. In a matter of seconds it was tied tightly.

When all the movement had ceased, she could hear herself breathing.

"Now your hands."

"Why?" She heard herself ask before she had time to stop herself from saying anything at all.

Instead of saying anything, the clown just stared at her. His red lips were curled downwards in an angry grimace, his black-circled eyes wide with fury.

She held her hands out, and allowed them to be tied as her legs had been.

When he was finished and standing – crouching – in the middle of the tent, Chloe could no longer feel the cold air slicing at her skin. Actually, when she thought about it, she hadn't felt cold for a while. It was as though the fear had boiled her blood, heated it and sent it burning through her body, eradicating the ice-cold slashes the night air had delivered that night.

Chloe heard a zip, and looked towards the entrance of the tent, expecting to see the other clown there.

But the tent was untouched. Nobody was standing there. Another zip had been pulled down.

Chloe reluctantly turned her head. The clown was on his knees, and struggling once again with Connor.

"What the-"

"Keep still."

"What the fuck are you doing?!"

Chloe heard the familiar sound of trousers being pulled down, and watched the clown climb on top of Connor.

She turned her head away and tried not to listen, tried to drown everything out with her sobbing; but the sounds of Sarah and Connor screaming in pain and horror carried through the night air, partnered with the cries of pleasure from the two madmen who held them captive in the forest.

*

It was just the two of them again now.

Connor's breathing was still heavy, and he was sometimes making strained noises of pain, still hurting from his horrifying encounter with the tall clown.

Neither of them had spoken since he'd left the tent.

Chloe dropped onto her side and wriggled as close to Connor as she could.

"Connor?" She whispered.

"I'm okay." He managed.

She didn't know what else to say, and she guessed that he didn't either.

Outside, she could hear the clowns speaking. They had been for the past few minutes. But now the sounds of a struggle had returned; Josh was being dragged outside.

"Here you go, boss."

Whatever the small clown had handed the tall one, it made Josh begin to whimper like a wounded canine.

"NO!" He screamed, and then there was a resounding *chop!*

His scream and the sound that had followed echoed through the trees.

How has nobody at the tour heard this? Chloe thought, and begin to consider screaming and shouting as loud as she could. However, she knew that she would be quickly silenced by the clowns; and if the noises so far that night hadn't alerted anyone's attention, she would surely fail. And when she thought about it, it *had* been quite loud at the attractions; people talking and screaming was a common part of the horror-themed event. Even if the sounds of the captives' clearing were making their way to the tour, why would anyone become suspicious of it?

"Do you want to take this one?" Chloe heard the tall clown ask.

"Oh, yes please, boss. Yes please!" Came the child-like response.

Chloe quickly rolled over onto her front, and wriggled forwards towards the entrance of the tent. Although she had no way of unzipping it, there was a tiny hole at the bottom which hadn't been zipped. She pushed her face as close to it as she could and looked out.

She couldn't see much – one eye made it difficult, and the size of the hole wasn't very revealing. She could see figures moving, looking at something on the ground. Chloe knew this was Sarah, but couldn't see her.

One of the figures was holding something above their head, something that gleamed in the light of the tree-lamp. It was brought crashing down swiftly, and before it hit its target the shining, silver object, like the dazzling rays of the sun, blinded Chloe as it reflected the light directly into her line of vision.

Chop! Chop!

...

Chop!

Then, out of the light, stomping towards the tent like a demon from the fires of hell, came the white-faced clown; his long legs striding, his red shoes flicking dirt across the ground, his long arms reaching out towards the tent.

"Your turn!" He beamed as he thrust his head into the tent.

Chloe wanted to grieve over the loss of her friends, to cry for them and remember all of the good times they'd had together. But now Connor's life was in danger, her life was in danger. Their baby's life was in danger.

She rolled onto her back again and quickly wriggled into the position she had been when the clown had left the tent.

The tall clown rushed in, breathing quickly and looking horrifically delighted.

"It's a shame," He sighed, "You two would have made beautiful children." He began to chuckle; a low, deep sound. Chloe's hand automatically went to her belly and rested on it, and she met eyes with Connor, who looked frighteningly scared.

The clown immediately turned his attention towards Connor again, and bent down, grabbed his legs and started to drag him out of the tent. Connor struggled, wriggled and fought against the clown; kicking out with both of his legs, forcing the clown to back off and even drop his grip at one point. The clown decided to change tactics; he walked over Connor's body and lifted him up into a sitting position, wrapped his arms around his body, stood him and then shoved him out of the tent with the speed of lightning and the power of thunder.

"No!" Chloe screamed, and threw herself forwards, trying to escape the tent.

She was blocked by a red shoe stamping only centimetres away from her hand.

Her chest suddenly became pained; her heart felt as though it had stopped beating. She let her head slump to the ground, and relaxed her body. Tears formed but she closed her eyes to stop them from streaming out.

She felt a hand drop onto her head, which then started stroking her hair. She felt repulsed; all she wanted to do was force the hand away, scream at the killer clown and fight against him to try and get away with Connor.

But she couldn't.

"You just stay here." He whispered, "I won't be long."

He left the tent and zipped it back up.

Chloe felt numb. She rolled over once again towards the back of the tent, and she stared at the thin, blue material above her.

"I'm pregnant." She said to him.

She saw his face; his blue eyes light up, his lips quickly turn into a smile.

Chop!

"I love you." She spoke aloud.

She heard footsteps stomping on the forest ground once again, and as she heard the tent unzipped, she turned her head and saw the tall, thin silhouette standing against the light. It stepped forward.

"I'm pregnant." She said to him.

She saw his face; the delight from his black-circled eyes disappear, his lips part in shock.

*

Jackson opened his eyes. This time, they stayed open.

He could still see his sister's glassy eyes staring at him through the trees of Wald Forest.

He blinked the images away and looked around the tent. It was just him now – no clowns.

Slowly, to make sure he didn't pass out again, he lifted himself up. When he was sitting up, he listened carefully. There were no sounds. How long had he been out? He guessed hours, but it was still dark outside; the light he could see appeared to be artificial.

He reached inside his jacket and searched his harness, which unsurprisingly now contained no equipment. He didn't have his phone, either, but he'd probably dropped that after his first encounter with the killer clowns.

As slowly and as quietly as he could, he got to his feet and began making his way towards the front of the tent. He pressed his ear up against the blue material and could still hear nothing. He decided now was as good a time as any to act.

He unzipped the tent quickly and stepped outside.

He saw the red splashed across the forest ground amongst dismembered, mutilated bodies and quickly looked away.

He was too late.

But he could still catch them.

The short clown was on his knees, amongst the bodies and appeared to be cleaning. Jackson was done with sneaking around and being cautious; he wanted these sick bastards to pay. He ran forward, the short clown heard him and turned around, but it was too late for him to move. Jackson leapt through the air, arms outstretched and tackled the clown to the ground, away from the bodies.

Jackson pinned the clown to the ground by holding his shoulders down, but the clown struggled against Jackson's grip, and it started to weaken. Jackson let go with one hand and sent his fist crashing into the middle of the clown's face, making his thick skin shake and face paint smear across Jackson's fist.

As Jackson pulled his fist back to strike again, something hard was driven between his legs, and he couldn't help but topple off the clown, gripping his groin in pain as he rolled to the floor. He clenched his teeth and pressed his eyelids shut, but quickly tried to get to his feet again, only for the pain to shoot into his stomach and him to fall down again.

He opened his eyes, expecting to see the clown coming in for another attack.

However, all he could see was the round figure of pinstripes running away into the trees.

"Fuck." Jackson growled.

Cox.

Was he still here?

The short clown was only the sidekick – Jackson could deal with him another time. Cox the clown was the main villain in all of this, and so he was Jackson's priority. Taking the killer clown down would also mean the end of the corrupt copper that was his Father.

Jackson heard talking.

He looked to the right and for the first time noticed the dark shadows moving around inside one of the blue tents.

Cox the clown was still there, and one of his intended victims was still alive.

*

"What?" He asked, his axe falling to the floor just before he dropped to his knees.

Chloe felt tears begin to drop from her eyes, "I'm p-p-pregnant." She squeaked, and lifted her hands up and wiped her face as best as she could.

He came towards her and reached for her hands, she retreated.

"No." He said urgently; a sudden change of tone from his calmness the rest of the night, "Just… I'm not going to hurt you… Just give me your hands."

Reluctantly, she held her hands out to him. What other choice did she have?

To her surprise, he freed her hands from the rope that bound them.

"Pregnant?" He asked, and smiled.

She nodded, and for the first time saw just how young the clown was. His face paint was now smudged and had clearly been dripping off with his sweat. He must have been only a few years older than Chloe, early to mid-twenties.

"Why?" Chloe asked, "Why are you doing this?" She clarified.

The clown's gaze dropped, "My… Mother…"

"What?" Chloe pressed, knowing the clown's position of power had been stripped from him now. Clearly revealing her pregnancy to him had worked in the way she had intended it to.

"My Dad killed her. I saw it. I remember it."

Chloe reached out and touched his hand, "I'm sorry." She said, and saw that the bald-headed, black-bearded man was now slowly making his way into the tent, sneaking up behind the clown.

"He's important… A policeman…" The clown continued, his eyes looking far away into the past, "She… Well, he helped her. She… with men, for money. You know?" He looked up quickly to check that she understood, and she nodded to show that she did. "I won't do that to a woman."

Chloe now understood why the young murderer had jumped to her defence earlier that night against the other clown.

"I… Sometimes, I want to try and be more like her. You look like her, you know?" He smiled but still didn't look at Chloe.

Chloe felt vomit rising, but tried to hold it back – that's why he'd done what he had to Connor and not to her; he wanted to be like his Mother. He'd also explained why she and her friends had been taken by him into the forest that night; Chloe reminded him of his Mother.

He reached out towards her belly, "This baby-"

She flinched and moved backwards. He finally looked at her, and his eyes showed the hurt he felt from her sudden and clear disgust and hatred for him.

"Fuck you." Chloe spat, as the bald man drove the wooden handle of the axe into the back of the clown's head.

Chapter Five

"He's on his way."

"Thanks." Jackson nodded, "The girl?"

"Chloe?"

"Is that her name?"

"Yes, Sergeant. She's still over at one of the ambulances. They're just checking her."

"And she really is pregnant?"

"Looks that way."

"Okay, thank you."

"What did you learn?" The PC asked.

"The clown is Cox's son. Sounds like he watched him kill his Mother when he was young. She was a prostitute who Cox had tried to help, but couldn't. No wonder he's so fucked up. By the sounds of it he rapes the males that he takes into the forest. He wants to be more like his Mother. And because he has so much 'respect' for women he won't rape them."

"Jesus…"

"Cox has been protecting him since the last murders."

"I'd heard the rumours about him but… to do this?"

Jackson shook his head, "Any sign of the other clown yet?"

"Sorry, JJ. Nothing."

Jackson patted the PC on the shoulder and walked past him, out of the trees and towards one of the ambulances which was parked alongside them.

Jackson had called the station after apprehending Cox the killer clown; officers, he was told, then shut down the 'Southumberland-Wald Forest Halloween Tour' for that night, sent everyone home and followed Jackson's directions to the clearing.

The girl he'd saved seemed dazed, and barely able to understand what was happening. Jackson carried her all the way through the trees and to the ambulance, occasionally looking down at her to make sure she was still conscious. Jackson was directed to the ambulances outside of the forest by the ambulance crew who came into the clearing along with the police officers to examine the bodies. Of course, he had almost immediately recognised the girl from earlier that night. She still looked beautiful, despite the shock that had gripped her face and glazed her eyes.

As Jackson approached the ambulance now, he saw that Chloe was more alert and actually communicating with the ambulance crew.

"Chloe, isn't it?" Jackson smiled at her. She was sat in the back of the ambulance. The crew moved away slightly to allow Jackson to speak to her.

She nodded.

He climbed into the back of the ambulance, "You were brilliant tonight, Chloe." He dropped to his knees and put a hand over hers.

"What's your name?" She asked, her voice weak and barely audible.

"James. James Jackson." He told her.

"James James Jackson?" She managed a slight laugh.

"Just James Jackson." He smiled.

"*You* saved *me*, Mr. Jackson. *You* were brilliant."

"And you probably saved dozens of people from that maniac," He assured her, "If it wasn't for you distracting him like you did I wouldn't have been able to take him alone… I thought… You were making the pregnancy up as a way of distracting him."

She shook her head.

Jackson didn't ask about the Father – he already knew the answer.

"Did you hear everything he said?" Chloe checked.

"I did. That was a big help. Now we understand why he's… like this. And we both heard it – we can both give statements now about what we heard… and saw, of course." Jackson quickly regretted adding that last part about giving statements; it was something that needed to be done but it wasn't something that should be said to someone who'd only just been rescued from the hands of a murderous psychopath. However, Chloe just nodded. Seemingly she'd already expected this.

Chloe had recovered quite quickly and was talking and asking more questions than Jackson was used to from someone in her position. He felt that there was a bond between them – one probably formed from her helping him catch the killer clown, and him saving her life.

"You will be given all the support you need, Chloe. I promise."

"Thank you, Mr. Jackson."

He waved a hand, "No need to keep being formal. You stay here, I'll be back to check on you later."

She nodded and smiled.

Jackson turned around. More red and blue, screeching sirens were approaching. He knew who it was, and stepped onto the pavement and watched the car stop outside the trees. The PC Jackson had been talking to earlier met Jackson's gaze, and Jackson just nodded. He looked back to Chloe who was now being tended to by the ambulance crew again; he was doing this for her, her baby and the Father who had been brutally taken from them that night.

Detective Sergeant James Jackson walked towards the police car and watched as Deputy Chief Constable Ralph Cox exited the back of the vehicle.

"Jackson."

"Sir."

"Why was I called here?" The tall man sniffed, acting as casually as he could.

"Your son is currently inside the forest." Jackson stated, "Being arrested."

Cox looked down at him, and his face drooped, his wrinkles showing more clearly.

"Deputy Chief Constable Ralph Cox, you are under arrest."

The veteran policeman wasted no time and prepared to strike, but Jackson had expected it. He gripped Cox's fist in mid-air and twisted forcefully. The old man grunted in pain and was forced to turn around to relieve the pressure being put on his aging bones, allowing Jackson to handcuff him.

"Take him away." Jackson said, and allowed the PC he had been talking to earlier to take over. "Ralph?" Jackson said mockingly, using his boss' first name as a sign of disrespect.

The tall man was turned around by the PC.

"Happy Halloween." Jackson smiled, mocking Cox further with his own words earlier that day.

Cox was turned back around, his eyes alight with rage, and put back in the rear of the car he arrived in. As Cox was sat down, his barely conscious son was walked out of the forest by more police officers.

Jackson looked at his boss, and saw the bitter glare he gave his son. Jackson turned his attention to the other Cox, who smiled sinisterly at his Father before being put into a police car himself.

Jackson looked back at Chloe, who was now lying down in the back of the ambulance and so thankfully hadn't had to look again at the clown who had taken her friends and boyfriend from her that night.

Jackson sighed and looked back at the trees.

Bodies in Wald Forest…

They had been avenged.

Tornwich – The Interlude

1. Local Hero

James Jackson walked through the corridors of the station and towards his office. The whole building had a different atmosphere these days; it was as though the dark cloud of corruption that had been looming over it had been lifted with Cox's downfall on Halloween night all those months ago. With his departure and the massive media coverage about his protection of his murderous son, a fast and frantic investigation was launched into the Southumberland Constabulary, and almost a quarter of the staff and officers employed by it found themselves dismissed or suspended and facing arrest for their involvement with Ralph Cox's dark and dodgy deeds which were exposed by the media and the investigation.

Despite all the good Jackson had managed to bring to his place of work, full justice hadn't been implemented. Former Deputy Chief Constable Ralph Cox was not in prison. It became evident to Jackson that Cox also had hidden friends within the legal system who were able to remain undetected by the media and the investigation, allowing them to make sure that he walked free, but were fortunately incapable of keeping him in his job.

Detective Inspector Hughes, however, had been imprisoned for his help in covering up the 'killer clown axe murders' as they were now being referred to by the media (so much for the 'Bunny-Man' copycat craze). With Hughes' departure and deserved punishment, Jackson had been promoted to Detective Inspector. Detective Inspector James Jackson quickly brought his old friend Andy onto his team, filling in Jackson's old role as Detective Sergeant; Andy was an effective worker as part of the team due to his experience from the 'Full Moon' Prom murders in Trexham that had taken place two years ago. Andy had thankfully long ago healed the mental scars from that case, and the experience he carried from it enabled him to be an enormous help in finalising the 'killer clown' case and put Ralph Cox's sinister son in prison.

Cox 'the killer clown', as Jackson referred to him, had been sent to a psychiatric hospital. During the court case, he became even more unhinged than he had been previously. He kept referring to his escaped victim, Chloe Clarke, as 'Mom'. He spoke about how he wanted to protect her child. Then, when asked quite directly about the horrors he had put Connor Morris through (as well as the male in his previous batch of victims), he, in a child-like manner, told of how he wanted to be like his 'Mommy'.

Jackson often felt it strange watching him without his clown costume or face paint on, but it allowed him to see the resemblance between him and his Father. He looked like a younger, more handsome version; and if Chloe really *did* look anything like his Mother, Jackson guessed that's where the looks came from. However, sometimes during the trial, usually when the jury and other onlookers were trying to stop themselves from gasping in horror as the atrocities that had been committed were described, Cox the killer clown would smile. His lips would curl into a grim grin, curling his eyebrows and darkening his eyes. Then, even in his natural state, he began to look more like the killer clown he'd been on that horrific Halloween night.

Jackson managed to have some interaction with Chloe while the trial was ongoing, but it was more limited than he would have liked it to be. She often seemed too much in a daze to talk, too traumatised by the terrors in Wald Forest to function naturally. Jackson hoped that she had recovered by now – surely her baby would be due soon, or already born and a few days old. Her family had seemed kind, caring and extremely supportive, and Jackson was confident that she was in good hands with her parents.

Chloe thanked Jackson every time they saw one another during the trial for saving her life, and he guessed the positive media coverage of him probably made her feel as though she was compelled to. 'Local Hero' was the caption beneath his picture in the paper after it was revealed how he brought both Cox the corrupt copper and Cox the killer clown to justice, saving a young lady's life.

Had he really saved Chloe's life, though? Was Cox the clown going to kill her? Probably not after she revealed she was pregnant, but surely he wasn't just going to let her go free. So Jackson had saved her from captivity, and probably many more lives that Cox would have taken as the horror tour continued to travel around Southumberland. But Jackson still felt some guilt. Connor. He had been too late to save Connor. Now Chloe's child was without one of its parents.

He thought about that case almost every day, even now. Most of all, he thought about Chloe and how much he wanted to see her again. He wanted to make sure her mental health was in good condition and that she and her baby would be able to do well together. He often fantasised about helping her, being there for her to help with her child, being there for her as Connor had been…

There was only ten years between them, he could have pursued it, but it just didn't feel right. The bond they had seemed to share in the aftermath of the Halloween of horrors seemed to have disappeared when the sadness of what had happened that night really sank in for Chloe.

He felt sad for her, too. He longed to see her again; he wanted to know that she was okay. Should he reach out? No. Too much time had passed now, it would just be awkward for him to do so now.

Not only that, but there were more reasons he shouldn't – *couldn't* – pursue a relationship with Chloe.

He'd had a relationship before, a woman he'd been with before becoming a sergeant. They had been together for a few years, all through his training, and it had been good. Well, more than good; he had loved her. He really had. Then, suddenly, after becoming a detective it had all changed. He hadn't even realised what was happening, but he was spending barely any time at all with Zoe. The time he was spending with her was whenever he got home from work and she was there. He couldn't imagine how that felt; hardly seeing the person you loved and them not even realising they weren't seeing you – as though you were invisible. If only he'd thought about that at the time.

It took him days to realise that he hadn't seen Zoe at all in almost a week, and that was when it had hit him. She'd given up. When he went home he noticed that everything of hers had disappeared, and the house was almost empty without her stuff there. He called her and apologised, tried to explain that he hadn't even realised what he'd been doing, but that just made her even more upset.

They met a few days later when Jackson had some spare time, but neither of them expressed interest in trying to make the relationship work. Jackson didn't hold back because he didn't love her or because he didn't want to be with her anymore, but because he didn't want to continue to hurt her. His new role consumed so much of his time that he hadn't even had chance to realise just how much time it was taking away from him. He didn't want to be with Zoe if he couldn't put her first; it would hurt both of them too much.

He didn't want to hurt Chloe in the same way he'd hurt Zoe.

Jackson was one of a handful of people at the Southumberland Constabulary who actually spent so much time on the job; many officers, detectives and other staff put hardly any effort in, usually those who were in the job for the wrong reasons or were part of Cox's corruption. But Jackson was there to, as simple and silly and child-like as it always sounded, stop bad things from happening. Seeing his sister lying dead in a forest had been all the motivation he'd needed to want to prevent anyone else from having to go through the same thing.

Jackson, sat at his desk, looked out the glass walls at the front of his office. Every time someone approached the door, he held his breath, for with Ralph Cox still walking free, and his murderous son's psychopathic companion still on the loose, Jackson didn't feel that he or anyone else involved with the events of that night were really safe.

2. Lone Survivor

Chloe, as she stood staring at the darkly engraved letters that made up the name of the man she had loved, felt a wetness begin to run down her leg.

She wiped the other wetness from her eyes and looked down at the lower part of her body that was wet; the liquid had gushed down her trousers and some of it was dripping onto the grass beneath her, underneath which was Connor's body.

"Oh, Chloe!" Her Mother whispered, with a slight sound of excitement in her voice.

After Connor's funeral, Chloe came to visit his grave as much as she possible could, which after a month or so turned into a weekly visit, which in turn had recently become a monthly visit.

Now, on her visit, it appeared her body had started the process of having their child. In that moment, as she looked down at the wet grass, her weak and tired mind was thankful that, in a way, Connor got to see her before she gave birth to their child.

She was having a boy. She found out as soon as she was able to, and she'd told Connor about it on her visit to him after she'd discovered the gender of their child. She thought Connor would have liked a boy.

"Mom?" She squeaked.

"It's okay love," Her Mom said, putting an arm around her and beginning to guide her away from the grave, "Let's get back to the car."

She wanted him to be with her. They should be together while the life they had made was brought into the world. She wanted to feel him wrap his arms around her and comfort her as they embarked on this new journey together.

But Connor was gone. That… *clown* had taken him away while she did nothing but cower and cry. She'd even done nothing while the clown inflicted what must have been the most traumatising, terrible part of that night upon Connor. That was the part that wouldn't leave her. The rest, she sometimes forgot, or could push to the back of her mind, but what the clown had done to Connor never left her for what felt like every single second of every single day.

She'd heard them. Heard the clown's cries of pleasure, heard Connor's screams of pain.

What had she done? Nothing.

What had she tried to do? Nothing.

Now, because of that, she was going to give birth to a fatherless baby. What if she'd told the clown earlier that she was pregnant? Maybe he would have spared Connor's life too… but surely he wouldn't have just let them walk free?

She had the policeman to thank for that, at least. The nice one, the honest one. Jackson. Of all the policemen she came across after that terrifying Halloween night, not one of them was as straight-talking or brutally honest as Jackson. The rest acted differently. Professionally. Although, she did have a feeling that Jackson's honesty was especially for her, albeit unintentionally. On that Halloween night, she had felt a bond between them. A bond that had been formed because he had saved her life, but she also felt a bond of truth in the aftermath of the horrors of Wald Forest. They had been open with one another, and Jackson had treated her fairly normally considering what she had been through, but she felt that Jackson's attitude was strangely more comforting than the people who were trying too hard to be delicate with her.

Chloe hadn't seen as much of Jackson as she'd have liked to after that night, and instead had to deal with professionals whose attitudes and treatment were more false than his. She didn't doubt the sadness they expressed when they apologised to her for the situation she was in, but if she was honest, that wasn't how she wanted people to act around her or what she wanted people to say to her.

She wanted Jackson.

She *wanted* Jackson.

She had felt he would stay in touch even after the case was over – he'd seemed to be that caring kind of person. But she hadn't seen him since.

She couldn't have Connor with her right now, but if she had to choose someone who could be, she'd choose Jackson.

He was similar to Connor. He didn't treat her as though she was a delicate little flower, a fragile snowflake that would fall to pieces if not handled with extreme care; he treated her just the same as any other person. That, she now realised, had probably been a huge reason as to why she had been so drawn to Connor in the first place when they had met at college almost two years ago now.

But now the case was over and Jackson was gone.

Perhaps he was too scared to stay in touch, suddenly treating her as the delicate object she did not want to be and felt she wasn't. Or, maybe, the special, honest treatment Jackson had given her was only intended to last the duration of the case.

However, she very much doubted the latter, although she wasn't sure if it was any better than the former.

"You okay, love?"

"Yeah, Mom."

The killer clown – what the newspapers called him – his face often haunted Chloe's nightmares. But not in his clown form, he always appeared the way he had in court. Dressed in a suit, with no face paint and no wild, green hair. The reason he appeared like this, Chloe deduced, was because the first time she had seen him in court had been much more terrifying than being trapped in the endless woodland maze of Wald Forest with him on Halloween night; because what had hit her seeing him in court for the first time was that he was not a blood-thirsty monster, a beastly creature or a bizarre alien. He was just a man.

His manner was calm as always, his actions calculated and deliberate. How could such a handsome, seemingly ordinary young man be such a brutal killer? (That's what some people were saying – namely those who brought him up when he was in a children's home – as quoted by some local magazines and newspapers).

But he was a brutal killer, and Chloe told the world exactly what he was; first in court, and afterwards in a statement to the media to try and crush the image of Cox the killer clown that other people were trying to create. He was branded as the 'killer clown', and after her contact with the media, she became more widely known as the 'Lone Survivor' – at least that was the caption underneath her picture in the newspaper.

Chloe suspected that the madman's 'important' Dad, as he had described him, had a part to play in trying to save his son as much as he could. He hadn't been able to save his son from prison, despite using his power and influence to do so for himself, so he had tried to orchestrate a scheme to create public sympathy for his son instead.

Ralph Cox was that man's name.

Was she in danger from him? She didn't think so; Jackson had assured her that Cox may have been corrupt, covered many murders and even committed one (that they knew of) himself, but he wasn't an psychopathic serial killer like his son – he wouldn't unnecessarily kill someone. His murder of his son's Mother had a reason behind it, as everyone had discovered during the case.

How was he walking free?

She'd read the news reports, but still didn't fully understand how.

He wasn't a threat, though, she was sure of that.

Because Jackson would protect her if he had to – she was sure of that, too. She'd seen the hate the Detective had for his old boss during the case.

Chloe looked out the window and saw the car pulling onto the hospital car park.

Her Mom, in what Chloe guessed was an attempt to distract her from what she was about to go through, asked a question that had been asked of her so many times throughout the last few months: "What are you going to call him then?"

"He'll have Connor's last name." Chloe replied; which had been her way of getting out of having to give a first name for so long, "Morris."

"The first name?" Her Mom tried, "Are you going to tell us that yet?"

Chloe sighed, and finally gave her answer.

"Jackson."

3. Outcast

Ralph Cox gripped the cubes of ice in his hand and let them slip slowly into the glass, one by one.

Clink.

'Ralph Cox'.

Clink.

That was all he was known as now.

Clink.

No more power.

No more 'Deputy Chief Constable'.

Just Ralph Cox.

The man whose son killed all those kids. The man who covered for his son who killed all those kids. The man who brought corruption to the Southumberland Constabulary – abusing his position to gain all the power he could; collusion with drug-dealing gangs, covering murders, corrupting fellow officers to rise through the ranks.

And he was the man who somehow got away with it all.

That, at least, still made him smile.

His final achievement.

He took his glass of ice-cold whiskey and walked out of the kitchen and into the living room, sitting down in front of the black, silent TV.

He had been so close to achieving what he'd always dreamed of: being Chief Constable. He had effectively been in control of everything for a number of years anyway with his connections and power, but it still would have been nice to have been given the title, to be the man walking out in front of the cameras to address the public…

He held his glass up to his lips, felt the coldness spread across them, and then quickly took a sip of the whiskey. The liquid slithered down his throat, the ice-coldness quickly burning into a wild, fire-like sensation.

It was *his* fault. Jackson.

He should have disposed of him a long time ago. He'd had the chances to do so, but always decided against it. Cox was powerful, yes, and respected because of his long tenure, but almost everyone in the Southumberland Constabulary had heard the rumours or knew about his dodgy deals and dark deeds. Those who weren't willing to go along with Cox or at worst no longer wanted to keep their mouths shut suddenly started to rally around Jackson; he had become a threat to his position very quickly, representing the opposite of what Cox did and becoming respected for it by those opposing Cox's methods.

It was *her* fault, too, though. The girl. Chloe.

Cox saw what his son saw – she *did* look like his Mother. But why show mercy? She was pregnant, sure, but Cox was willing to sacrifice those who stood in his way in a similar position to Chloe. His son's Mother, for example, killed when their child was so young. "No mercy." Cox whispered into his whiskey.

Had it all been for nothing?

IT WAS *HIS* FAULT. His son's.

He'd gotten in the way. Cox only covered for him out of a sense of duty… and, he supposed, fear. If he hadn't, and his son was caught, everything would have been revealed. But now it had, anyway.

"But I'm walking free." Cox smiled, and then chuckled, which quickly turned into a high-pitched, maniacal laugh. His head tilted back, leaning on the chair, his chest bouncing with each cackle.

Had it really been his final achievement, or had it been his last stand?

It would have all needed to end at some point anyway, wouldn't it?

He'd never know now, all because of his foolish, careless bastard of a son.

Cox suddenly stood from his chair.

His hand curled around the glass in his hand, before his arm reached back, tensed, and then propelled the glass forward and up against the wall above the TV. The glass crashed against the wall and shattered.

What did he do now?

He couldn't go out. Too many people would know his face from the papers; he'd already had all that trouble during the trial with death threats and people stalking his house. He couldn't even pursue his usual method of exacting revenge against those who had caused him trouble. His downfall. Nobody would want anything to do with him now, and he'd called in his last favours during the trial to make sure he wasn't imprisoned. He most certainly would not become a boring, retired old man and sit in the house all day watching the TV... but isn't that what he'd been doing for the past few months? No. That had been about keeping a low profile. Now was the time to *do something*.

But he couldn't. There was nothing for him now. No job, no family, no life.

He was an outcast.

So just what the fuck was he meant to do now?

4. Prisoner

He lay on his bed, hands behind his head, staring at the ceiling. It was a hot day – he could see the sun outside the tiny window, feel it on his face whenever he was up and walking about or looking out of the bars of the window. And yet, despite the summer heat, the place he was locked in always seemed cold. It was as though there was always an ice-cold wind that breezed through the halls and the walls, cutting his skin and whispering obscenities.

A 'psychiatric hospital', and they called him a 'patient'. He wasn't a patient, he was a prisoner.

Kill her, the wind whispered as it sliced across his cheeks.

He wasn't going to axe her like the others… maybe afterwards he would have, but not to kill her. He'd wanted to strangle her, because she'd looked so much like his Mother. He wanted to try and experience what his Father had on that night so long ago. But then she'd revealed that she was carrying a child, and he'd showed mercy.

With her boyfriend gone, and with her beginning to listen to him and allow him to confide in her, he felt that maybe they could have raised the baby together. He'd felt that they were bonding… but then she'd retreated when he tried to touch her.

"Fuck you."

That's what she'd said, and then everything went dark.

That Detective who his Father had warned him about. *Jackson.*

Why hadn't Ralph just disposed of him? He surely would have done it had it been anyone else causing him trouble, and the colour of Detective Jackson's skin should have been all the motivation his Father needed. But he thought he knew why Ralph hadn't disposed of Jackson; secretly, deep down, he wanted Jackson to catch him. He knew that the lifestyle he'd pursued made his Father… uncomfortable, and he probably wanted it to end almost as much as Jackson had.

He rolled off his bed and stood up. He walked over to the window and looked out; it was quite high up on the wall, and any average man would probably struggle to get up that high, but he could easily reach it standing normally and see outside.

The bright, warm rays of the sun shone across his face, but he couldn't feel them. In fact, he didn't want to feel them, he preferred the cold air of the 'hospital' slashing across his skin. Just like on that Halloween night when the freezing, ice-like air of Wald Forest had hung heavy around him and those he had taken.

The only time that night he'd felt any warmth was when he took Chloe's boyfriend. He just wanted to be like his Mom, that's why he did it to the men and not the women; he wouldn't inflict upon them what he'd seen so many men inflict upon his Mom in the short time he'd known her. Her boyfriend that night, though, he'd been one of the best looking men he'd ever seen…

He wished that he could see the child he and Chloe had made together, it would surely be beautiful.

And maybe he would see it, maybe sometime not too far in the future, because just maybe he would soon be out of the place he was being kept a prisoner in, and maybe he would find himself reunited with those who had ruined his life: Ralph, Jackson, Chloe, and that baby…

5. Clown

He remembered all their times in the children's home together. They had always had the urge to kill from a very young age; he could remember it very well. It was the reason both of them had bonded so quickly there. They had stayed up many nights, talking about why they were there and how they hated those responsible for them being there.

Quite soon their urges became apparent. They didn't yet express them physically, but told one another about their dark desires.

They didn't get to put their needs into action for a long time; a few years passed and they had set certain boundaries which prevented them from killing certain people. Fellow children at the home were off limits, or any children for that matter. The people who worked there were too nice and caring to be potential victims.

It wasn't until they were in their final year of high school that they finally got to do what they'd only dreamed of for so long. They went for a walk in the city centre of Tornwich one night, sneaking out of the home and taking knives from the kitchen with them. They'd had the idea for a while but only that night finally built up the courage to go out and do it.

They often noticed the people sleeping on the street in the city, people that nobody would miss, people that nobody would even realise were gone.

One of them was asleep on a park bench, and even though it was the first one they came across that night, they chose him and went in for the kill straight away. They clumsily stabbed and slashed at the struggling body, until they quickly became desperate and started stabbing places they knew were highly likely to result in a quick death before the man was able to get away from them.

This was an act they repeated only once more (a couple of months later), as rumours of a serial killer targeting homeless people started to circulate and they got anxious about slipping up and getting caught.

That second kill had been better, though. They knew what to expect that time and so had been more excited than nervous. There was still some mild panic when they were during the act, but the adrenaline that pumped through their bodies seemed to flush out the fear. Still, they knew they had to stop before a pattern emerged and suspicions were high, because the longer they continued to have a routine, the more likely it was that they were caught.

The next opportunity they got was the best one. Again, a couple of years of waiting was needed, but the 'Southumberland-Wald Forest Halloween Tour' served as the perfect outlet for the killings they so very desperately needed to commit.

But now it was over.

His friend Cox was gone, and it wasn't the same anymore.

He hadn't meant to run away completely; just make the Detective think he had and then come back to ensure he could be silenced. But very quickly sirens had sounded and police swarmed around the clearing where the blue tents were set up.

If he didn't think he would be caught long before he attempted it, he would head towards the psychiatric hospital where he knew Cox was, set him free and seek vengeance upon all those who were responsible for the position they were in now. That Detective would surely be first – Jackson. Although he had been easy to knock down that night – he'd managed to do so more than once – it was his ability to keep getting back up and their lack of preparation for that which played a huge part in their downfall.

Maybe he could still attempt his plan for revenge, or maybe he would just stick with what he was doing right now.

Cox had been the killer clown – the papers said so – and he was just the 'accomplice'. But now he was the one creating fear, making people feel uncomfortable in the knowledge that he was still on the loose, he was the clown now.

He had been hiding out in the cellar of a house for the past few weeks, and he felt that he knew the family above well enough now to be able to ensure he captured them all before killing them. He knew how many of them there were, their names and their routine. He was ready to strike. He had no axe this time, but there were plenty of tools in the cellar that he could put to use.

He already had the chairs lined up in the cellar, the tape on the side with his 'tools' which were looking shiny and sharp after his work on them.

Slowly, he began the ascent up the cellar stairs and into the house, knife in hand…

PART TWO

'Justice has at last been served,

But the public are still unnerved,

Once again it is Halloween night,

And they're all in for a fright.'

Chapter Six

Chloe heard her phone ringing in the other room. She made sure Jackson was asleep before she left the room and quickly rushed downstairs to grab her phone. She didn't like to leave him on his own at all, even though she knew he wasn't going to get up and go anywhere and he was pretty much incapable of hurting himself. She picked up her phone – it was lying on the living room sofa – and looked at who was calling her. Lincoln. She tapped the green button on the screen and held the phone up to her ear while rushing back up the stairs to her bedroom.

"Lincoln?" She managed to breathe out as she bounded up the stairs, her legs stretching from step to step.

"Chloe! Hello sexy girl." He said in a deep, low voice. She could hear in his voice that he was trying to do the 'cool boy' act that she thought boys got rid of after high school. She hadn't met anyone like it in college, but now that she had started university and met Lincoln, she saw that she was wrong.

"Fuck off. Do you actually want anything or just to harass me some more?" She reached her bedroom and looked down at Jackson, who was still sleeping peacefully, "And be quiet, Jackson is asleep." She tried as much as she could to bring Jackson into their conversations; she always hoped that having a child would deter Lincoln, but it never did.

"Aw, how is the little man?"

"Fine." *Fucking scum,* she thought. To anyone else, he would sound like a caring, thoughtful young man. That was the image he tried to put across, and often succeeded, but Chloe knew that he wasn't actually like that.

"Am I going to get to see you tonight then?" Lincoln asked.

"No, thank you." This wasn't the first time she'd told him 'no' to meeting up. In fact, she'd lost count of the amount of times that he'd phoned her or seen her at university, asking if they could do something together. She would always reject him. At first, she'd been delicate, especially if he was around his friends, not wanting to embarrass him. Eventually, though, she became too annoyed to care and started being more abrupt with him, let him down gently clearly wasn't working. She found that even though his friends would make jokes if they were present, it never deterred him. She even thought that it probably motivated him even more; he wanted to prove them wrong and show that he could 'get her', she was a challenge she guessed.

"Go on." He pushed.

"Lincoln, there are hundreds of other girls at university, why don't you go and pester them? I'm sure they'd love it if you called them." Lincoln *was* good-looking, she had to admit that, and with him studying sports at university he had the body to go with it as well. The 'cool boy' act was probably attractive to a lot of girls, too, but not to her. It was a shame she hadn't seen that side to him when they'd first met or she'd never have given him any of her time.

"Oh, no doubt they would." Chloe could almost feel his cocky smile just through the phone, "But it's you I want." There it was again. Why did he do it? It was an act, surely? Why couldn't he just be his normal self as he had been when they'd first met? Unless *that* was the act, and *this* was the real him, she considered.

"I'm going, Lincoln." She said firmly, but knew that it would have no effect. Sometimes, when she let herself think about it for long enough, she wondered how long it would be before his attitude started to escalate and become more dangerous and she would have to call the police. Maybe that wouldn't be such a bad thing...

Jackson.

"See you soon."

"Whatever." *See? He just can't take no for an answer.* She involuntarily rolled her eyes.

"Happy Halloween."

The phone buzzed as he hung up, but his parting words left her stunned and motionless. She knew what day it was, but had tried (mostly successfully) to push it to the back of her mind and carry on with her daily routine as though it was any other ordinary day.

This time a year ago she would have been making plans with Connor and her friends to go out to the 'Southumberland-Wald Forest Halloween Tour'. She knew they shouldn't have gone to it. She had a bad feeling about it because of the murders in Wald Forest earlier that month. But she'd thought that she was being silly and just carried on with the day. She should have trusted her initial instinct.

She sighed and threw her phone onto the bed. She turned to Jackson and checked on him. He was in the same position he had been when she started the phone call. She reached down and lightly stroked the strands of light blond hair on his head – he was bound to have that colour hair seeing as both Chloe and Connor had it. His eyes were blue, too, and she thought she could already tell that he was going to have the eyes of his Father.

She turned away from him and sat down on the edge of her bed, picking her phone back up and holding it in her hands, staring at the black screen, half expecting a message or another phone call to come through from Lincoln.

She had met Lincoln in the first week of university when introductory events were held in place of classes during the day and 'student nights' were held in nightclubs in the city during the evenings and going on into the early hours of the next morning. Chloe wasn't really one for partying, but seeing as she was living at home and not on-campus, she decided that she had to take every opportunity she could to meet fellow students and make friends.

On her first 'student night', she'd gone to a nightclub with some friends she'd made from her introductory session a day earlier. It was on that night that she met Lincoln Brooks and his friends.

She'd left Jackson at home with her parents, who were more than happy to look after him for the night, and had even encouraged her to go out and 'have a break' as they'd put it. She was slightly reluctant to do so, but knew that she should take the opportunity, and so did.

She had found the night very refreshing, and could instantly see the way Lincoln was looking at her, and she guessed he could also see the way that she was looking at him. He'd seemed nice at first, very genuine, and she enjoyed talking to him. He was studying sports and lived on-campus, she quickly discovered as they exchanged the familiar student pleasantries, asking one another what they are studying, where they come from and all the other banalities of small talk that Chloe hated, but were somehow necessary as a prelude to any conversation at university it seemed. Late in the night, when the conversation had easily transitioned onto more interesting topics, they both left the nightclub and went back to his student flat.

When he took his jacket off, she saw that he was quite muscular and had a big, broad chest. He took his shirt off and walked over towards her. Without thinking, she reached out towards his body and ran her hands across his skin, feeling the firmness beneath it. Then, he had reached down and took her shirt off, feeling her chest as she had his.

She lay down on the bed and he climbed on top of her. She looked into his dark, brown eyes and ran a hand through his spikey, black hair before placing a hand across his cheek, feeling his rough stubble. He was very different to Connor, almost the opposite, especially in terms of hair and eye colour, spikey, gelled hair instead of short and combed and he was more muscular, too. When she thought about it, she'd never really had a 'type', and so tried not to let herself think about it too much.

However, all through the night, she had found herself constantly comparing him to Connor, but she guessed that was normal – Connor was the only 'real' relationship she'd ever had.

She didn't feel bad or guilty about what she was doing. She had to move on – everyone had told her that and she knew it was true. Connor, she knew, wouldn't want her to live an isolated, lonely, boring life. So she had taken everyone else's advice and done what she thought Connor would have wanted her to (as clichéd a line as that was, she knew it to be true), but she had done it in her own time.

She only came to regret what she'd done when Lincoln became extremely and annoyingly clingy. Neither of them were in a relationship or wanted one at the time – they had made that clear to one another. But then Lincoln started trying to treat her as his girlfriend whilst simultaneously claiming he still didn't want one and was constantly doing his 'cool boy' act. They had only slept together that one night, and Chloe kept it that way, despite Lincoln's constant pressing for an encore.

Eventually, Chloe did want another long-term boyfriend, but she wanted someone who was more mature than Lincoln.

She thought he had been, at first, which is a reason why she hadn't regretted sleeping with him. Now, though, she almost thought of it as a disgrace to Connor's memory. A thought she tried not to dwell on too much, or she knew it would consume her and upset her.

Still, she wished she had waited longer before sleeping with someone at university, even if they had turned out to be nice as Lincoln had seemed at first. She should have got to know someone better and tried to form a proper relationship – but that was another problem; did she really want a serious relationship while she was going through university? It was probably best that she didn't. She decided she wouldn't actively seek one, at least, but if it found her, then why not go for it?

Unfortunately, Lincoln was certainly not someone for the long-term.

So, for now, she would focus on her studies and on Jackson.

Boys could wait.

Chloe unlocked her phone and saw that her Dad had text her: *Me and your Mom are going for something to eat after work, will you be okay at home for a couple of hours tonight? Your friend is still coming round, isn't she?*

She rolled her eyes and began to type her reply, she'd already told her parents that Abby was coming round, and they'd hinted that they might go out but weren't sure about what to do. She knew why – they didn't want to leave her alone on Halloween, but she'd tried her best to make it clear she'd be fine with Abby. She didn't want to be stifled and overprotected because of what had happened, she preferred to carry on as normal. She read over her reply before hitting 'send': *I'll be fine thanks, Dad. Yeah, I've asked Abby round for a couple of hours anyway. I'll see you later.*

She opened her contacts, clicked on the name 'Abby' and then the call option that appeared beneath her name before putting the phone to her ear.

Abby was the first friend she'd made at university. They met in quite a similar way to how Chloe had first made friends with Sarah at college. On the first day of the first week of university, in the introductory session the her English degree, she'd sat next to Abby and they had gone through the usual necessities of asking where they were each from, and it turned out they lived fairly close to one another.

It wasn't long before Chloe confided in Abby about her past and current situation; as it turned out, Abby already knew, having read the news months earlier, but didn't realise that Chloe was the girl she had read about. So when October arrived and Halloween started to approach, Abby had suggested coming over to Chloe for a couple of hours and 'maybe a drink or two'. They were always visiting one another's houses after becoming friends, and so Chloe didn't see this as special treatment because of the significance of Halloween night to her, but rather just a friendly meet-up.

Abby actually reminded Chloe a lot of Sarah, but without a Josh. She even spoke similarly, had the same fashion sense and had the same attitudes to most things; it was as though

Sarah had never gone anywhere, but paradoxically, most of the time it just served as a reminder that Sarah *was* gone. Not that Chloe needed to be reminded, she thought about her old friend every day regardless.

Ring, ring.

Ring, ring.

Click.

"Chloe! You okay?"

"Good thanks, still coming round later?"

"I am indeed! I'll bring a bottle."

"Lovely. I have got Jackson though."

"We're not going to be getting smashed, Chloe."

Chloe laughed, "Fair enough, then!"

"How are you?" Abby asked, but the question had an odd tone to it, and Chloe knew that Abby was probably referencing what day it was.

"Lincoln called me. Again." Chloe replied, acting as though it was any other day, as she had been so far.

"He's going to have a fucking punch from me one of these days, you know? What did he want this time, the fucking creep?"

"The usual. Asked if I wanted to 'do something' with him tonight."

"You told him to fuck off I assume?"

"Exactly those words."

"Good."

"He'll still probably invite himself round at some point."

"Well, I'll be there with you, so we can take him together."

Chloe smiled, but then thought about Jackson, "I like to think we could! I really don't want any trouble with Jackson in the house though."

"Why don't you give the other Jackson a call?" Abby suggested, her voice going slightly high-pitched, as though she knew she was being bold in her recommendation.

"I don't have his number."

"Then go to the police station."

"I can't just walk in there like that!"

"Of course you can, I'm sure he'd love to see you."

Chloe remained silent.

"I know you want to."

"Well of course I want to!"

"Would be hilarious to watch him take out Lincoln."

The image of Jackson wrestling Lincoln to the ground on her front garden made her smile, but she knew she wouldn't be seeing Jackson.

"I could go for you." Abby continued to press.

"Abby! This isn't high school!"

"Fine!" She sighed, "You just carry on lusting after a man who you're not going to even bother talking to and carry on dealing with Lincoln."

"We'll just deal with it as it happens." Chloe replied, "If he does come round, you'll be here and so will my parents, probably."

"Probably?"

"They're going out for something to eat after work."

"Probably best they aren't there, then we can fight Lincoln properly."

"Abby!" Chloe shouted, but smiled, because she could hear the humour in Abby's voice, "My Dad would probably knock him out anyway."

"Oh God, your Dad doesn't know about him?"

"Of course he does."

"What did he say?" Abby asked, as though expecting Chloe to detail how her Dad had scolded her for 'sleeping around' – the typical response that most parents would probably have to her situation.

"Just that if he ever steps foot near the house he'll kill him."

"What about… you know… your 'interactions' with Lincoln?"

"Well, I didn't really run through the details with my *FATHER*. But he knows, and he didn't really say anything. Even if he did have something to say it wouldn't matter, I'm a grown woman for fuck's sake."

"I know, I know, it's just weird. My Dad would probably slap me."

"Well he wouldn't have any right to."

"I know, but he probably would."

"What time are you thinking of coming round anyway?"

"Hm." Abby replied thoughtfully, "Around the time the trick or treaters start taking to the streets. So… a couple of hours? Evening?"

"Sounds good!"

"Amazing. I'll see you later."

"See you later." Chloe said cheerfully, already eagerly anticipating her friend's arrival later that day.

But, due to events that became all too frighteningly familiar to those that occurred last Halloween, she never did see or even speak to Abby again…

*

Detective Inspector James Jackson could see someone approaching his door out of the corner of his eye. He continued tapping at his keyboard, not wanting to acknowledge them until he had to, still fearing that every time someone had something to tell him it was to do with the 'Cox the Killer Clown' case.

Today made it even worse – Halloween – it was the anniversary of that horrific night.

This time a year ago he would have been doing what he was doing now; sat at a desk, typing on a computer, thinking about the steps he was going to take in order to apprehend the 'Bunny-Man Copycat' as everyone thought it was at the time.

Knock, knock.

"Come in." Jackson ordered, and reluctantly switched his gaze from his computer monitor to the doorway, which was now occupied by Andy rather than the glass door that usually took up the space.

"Boss!" Andy breathed, as though he'd run to Jackson's office and was in a rush to convey some important news.

Sensing the urgency, Jackson got to his feet, "What is it?"

"JJ," Andy sighed, suddenly seeming hesitant to say what he had so eagerly come to.

Jackson walked from behind his desk and in front of Andy, whose head was becoming filled with beads of sweat; his eyes looked scared and anxious, his mouth quivered, as though trying to speak but the words were refusing to form. "Andy, what is it?" Jackson said, more slowly this time, letting Andy see that he *needed* to know what had happened.

"You need to come with me, JJ." Andy finally managed.

"What's happened?" Jackson demanded, hearing the volume of his voice suddenly rising, seeing heads turning his way from outside his office.

"JJ… Just come with me, please." Andy turned and starting to speedily walk out of the office.

Jackson followed quickly, knowing that something *bad* had happened. He wasn't sure how, but deep down he already knew – it must have been Andy's urgency, combined with clear reluctance to convey whatever information he had – he knew that something had happened to sinisterly commemorate what had happened on Halloween night last year.

*

Abby set her phone down on the bedside table and rested her head on her pillow.

She knew Chloe probably didn't want to talk about what day it was and what had happened on this day last year, but she also wanted her to open up, knowing it wouldn't be healthy for Chloe to hold her thoughts and feelings in about it. She would get upset, undoubtedly, but Abby reasoned that it would be better for Chloe to release her demons rather than allowing them to possess her.

Maybe being alone together and some alcohol would loosen her up. Abby knew everything that had happened a year ago from reading about it and the little things Chloe had managed to tell her; she wasn't just being intrusive, she wanted to help her friend overcome what she still evidently hadn't.

It wasn't just last year that Abby knew was on Chloe's mind, though. There was much more. Lincoln, for a start, he wasn't being very helpful at all. *He must know about what happened to her,* Abby often thought to herself, but knowing what Lincoln was like she knew it was probably something that made him think it would be easier to take advantage of Chloe.

Abby, like Chloe, had thought Lincoln was a genuinely nice guy the first time they had met him just over a month ago. If she was being truthful, she even fancied Lincoln a little bit herself, and had told Chloe so; but there probably weren't many girls who *wouldn't* fancy Lincoln. It was his personality that was the problem.

Abby knew exactly what Chloe meant when she described Lincoln's 'cool boy' act, although the term Abby would probably use is 'bad boy'. The attitude had probably helped him in getting with many girls in high school, but in university Abby knew he would struggle to impress most girls with it. A handful would probably like it, but not girls like Chloe.

She rolled off the bed and onto her feet, and tapping her phone screen she saw that she still had a couple of hours to get ready before setting off to Chloe's, but decided she should probably get to the shops now and pick out a drink for them. She snatched her phone up from the table and sped downstairs and into the kitchen, where she made sure everything she needed was inside her purse before putting it into her bag and slinging it over her shoulder.

She started to head down the hall corridor when she remembered she hadn't locked the back door or picked up her keys. She returned to the kitchen and saw that the back door was open. She hadn't left it open... had she?

Suddenly, a sound came from behind her, metal sliding on metal.

Her eyes fell on the knife block where she saw that one of the knives was missing, her breath caught in her throat and she quickly turned around. That was a decision she instantly regretted; she should have ran straight out of the back door she thought, but now it was too late, and she knew it. Her body seemed to betray her and give up there and then, her knees buckling as all the strength seemed to leak from her legs.

From across the room, the man in the clown mask sped towards her; not running, but walking *very* quickly – his knife held high in the air.

Blood-red, circular nose, dark blue lips curled into a huge frown rather than a joyful smile, black-rimmed eyes that were exposed (the only part of the face not covered by the plastic). They were wide with... what? Rage? Excitement? Madness?

The all-in-one clown costume was split down the middle: one side black, the other orange in what were typical Halloween colours.

Time seemed to be going in slow motion as she observed all of this in fractions of seconds; the figure covered the space between the two of them at a furious speed and a slight scream that was actually more of a squeak was all that she could muster as the figure slashed his knife across her face.

She felt a burning pain across her eyes, cheeks and mouth. Blinded, she fell backwards and landed hard and painfully on her back.

The last thing she heard was the man's heavy breathing beneath the mask, like an excited dog playing with a half-dead animal.

The last thing she felt was the man's hand force her, by the throat, forcefully flat on the cold kitchen floor.

The last thing she saw was the flash of light on steel lifted high above her prone form.

Then, the knife crashed into her chest.

Then, nothing.

Chapter Seven

"Have you ever heard of Landon Barker?" Andy said as he and Jackson both exited their cars at the same time.

Jackson knew the name, but with all the thoughts that were piling up inside of his mind right now, everything became jumbled and unrecognisable. He and Andy started walking towards the large building in front of them, its long and black windows like the dark eyes of one of the 'inmates' inside, stalking them silently and sinisterly. Jackson finally shook his head, knowing he recognised the name 'Landon Barker', but not being able to place it.

"He escaped from Ashmoor about twenty years ago? The cannibal teacher?" Andy tried, and Jackson started to remember the story, but let Andy carry on anyway, "He was a high school teacher, killed and ate some of his students and colleagues, they caught him eventually, but had barely held onto him for a few years before he escaped. Turns out he'd hidden in Wald Forest, coming across some unfortunate campers. There was only one survivor."

Jackson remembered fully now, "Something tells me you haven't brought me here because Landon Barker has finally been re-captured after all these years?" Jackson knew that Barker had never been found again after leaving his own 'lone survivor' behind, and as much as the families of his victims wanted justice (probably because they feared a return; especially the woman who had survived his second spree of killings), he had shown no signs of a third comeback in Southumberland or anywhere else, meaning there was simply no need to pursue him anymore after twenty years.

Andy was silent, and seemed to consider Jackson's words, before he shook his head. "No, we haven't caught him… That was just an example of…"

"What?" Jackson asked firmly, trying to show Andy that he wanted an answer quickly, he was losing his patience.

"It's what the papers will be comparing this to, Jackson, I know it. Not only this, but the Bunny-Man again… He escaped, remember?"

Again. Andy had said "again". What occurrence did Jackson know of that had been compared to the Bunny-Man before? Yes, he knew, and he was becoming very aware of the specific comparisons Andy was trying to draw his attention to.

Jackson nodded, "Yes, Andy, I know the *urban legend.*" He put emphasis on the last two words, trying to make sure that Andy hadn't lost his mind and started thinking that the Bunny-Man was real.

"I know, I know. It's not real." Andy confirmed, "But this is what they're going to draw comparisons to…"

Jackson already knew what had happened, and felt Andy was about to finally confirm it for him, but it still hit with such a force that it felt like he'd been kicked in the face as he had been on *that night* – twice – by the short, fat clown.

"The Bunny-Man escaped decades ago and took the Bridge as his home… Landon Barker escaped twenty years ago and slaughtered in Wald Forest… And now… Now Cox's son is out, JJ. They can't find him. His room was unlocked and he was just… gone… I'm sorry."

Jackson saw police officers waiting at the entrance of the psychiatric hospital and members of staff who worked there ready to greet him and Andy. Jackson already had his plan of action, though; he wasn't going to sit around talking and waiting for Cox the clown to strike, as would most likely be the plan of action. They would all probably sit and talk about Cox, how his mental state and behaviour had been recently, before saying there was nothing they could all do until he left a trace of evidence that would give up his whereabouts. Jackson knew what that meant – they had to wait for Cox to kill somebody before they could locate him. This time, at least, Jackson wasn't going to let that happen. He was going to – had to – get *there* before Cox the clown did.

"Andy. Call me if there's any developments." With that, Jackson turned around and jogged back to his car. Andy didn't shout after him, and Jackson didn't look back; Andy had probably expected this reaction, which is why he'd been so reluctant to tell Jackson what had happened.

Jackson practically threw himself into the driver's seat and began driving almost instantly, neglecting his seatbelt. It wasn't the first time he'd broken such a law that he was meant to enforce; sometimes though, in the rush of a situation, simple and small mistakes like it happened.

He started driving. He knew Chloe's address even now. He'd remembered it from before.

Cox the clown was bound to be heading to her. From experience, Jackson knew that he would blame her for what happened. Killers, as much as they liked attention, didn't like getting caught. That also meant they definitely didn't like anyone who had survived their terror.

Landon Barker. Tornwich's very own cannibal killer. Jackson could remember it clearly now; he'd only been a child at the time but had obviously learnt more about it serving in the Southumberland Constabulary. There were still those who remembered him at the station. It was something that had never been discussed in-depth, but Jackson had heard the case mentioned briefly, often in passing.

Now Ralph Cox's son. Tornwich's very own killer clown. Would this be the one that Jackson would remember for the rest of his life? The one that affects him as the 'Full Moon' Prom affected Andy? Imprints itself in his memory as Barker's cannibalistic killings had imprinted themselves on the memories of other officers?

Chloe was considered the 'lone survivor' of Cox's killings; Jackson left out of that grouping so the media could sell the story in a more Hollywood-style way, and brand him as the 'local hero'.

Barker had his lone survivor – she was still alive.

Jackson would stop at nothing to make sure that Chloe Clarke remained the lone survivor of 'Cox the Killer Clown'.

*

Chloe looked out of the window, it was already starting to get dark and it wasn't even evening yet. She probably still had another hour or two before Abby arrived. She turned her attention back to Jackson, who was seated on her knee and yawning. Chloe had woken him from his afternoon nap to feed him, and then change him before spending a little over an hour playing with him in her room.

"You're not tired again, already?" She asked, to which Jackson responded with a tired stare, and then a series of fatigued blinks, as though it was a massive strain just to close his eyes and open them again. She picked Jackson up and cradled him with her one arm, checking the time on her phone. "Okay," She sighed, "Maybe you can have an evening nap again today."

Jackson seemed to sleep almost all of the time. Chloe thought it was odd but her parents seemed to think it was normal, so she tried not to worry about it too much. She *had* read and heard about it during her pregnancy when she was preparing, but hadn't expected him to sleep *this* much.

Chloe looked at the framed photo of her and Connor on the bedside table. Connor never really slept very much. Even when they stayed up late after going out with Sarah and Josh or just had a night to themselves, going out for something to eat or staying in and watching a film. He would always wake quite early in the morning, but Chloe would always wake to find that he was still in bed next to her, sometimes on his phone, but mostly she would turn over in the bed to see him propped up on an elbow, stroking her back or her hair softly. She remembered the way his arm would tense slightly as he stroked, the muscle bulging slightly beneath the skin as it contracted with each movement, up to his shoulder and across his chest. The way she would shuffle in close to him, pressing her head against those muscles of his chest, feeling his light, blond hairs brush against her face.

When Chloe looked back on her night with Lincoln, everything seemed wrong now. *Everything*. She had woken to find him snoring like a giant zoo animal next to her. She'd moved in close to him, stroking the black hair of his chest only for him to moan in his sleep and roll over. Even now, the hair seemed the wrong colour to her (strange, she thought, seeing as she often thought of Detective Jackson – who had the some of the darkest, blackest hair she had ever seen; but they shared a different bond that went beyond physical attraction, they shared a bond from *that night*). The way he had turned away from her in his sleep now seemed like a bad omen. If only he'd turn away from her now, in a conscious state, and spare her from the memory of the night they spent together.

She almost felt as though she'd cheated on Connor. She had to move on, yes, and she'd accepted that. But Lincoln… Not the right person to do it with. She'd even apologised to Connor when she visited the cemetery after discovering what Lincoln was *really* like.

She found her mind drifting back once again to Jackson. Not her sleeping baby, but Detective Jackson. She realised often how little they actually knew of one another, but still she found herself thinking about him so much. Did he think about her? Maybe it was for the best that she never meet Jackson again, because maybe he would turn out just like Lincoln; not as nice as he'd first seemed.

But she knew that wasn't true. Jackson was good. She knew it.

She had seen how honest he was, she'd even read about it in the aftermath of *that night*. Jackson had managed to take down Ralph Cox, and all the corruption of the Southumberland Constabulary with him. And, even though it scared her, she saw the way he was afraid of the younger Cox just as she was. Except he was able to put on a much braver act than her. She had seen through it though, and that was where their connection lay. The bond they had formed through their experience of the events they had shared *that night*.

Chloe stood up and walked over to her bedroom window. It was very dark now, and some street lamps had already started to come on. It seemed trick or treating and some Halloween parties had already started, as many zombies, vampires and ghosts had taken to the street.

Chloe wished that Abby was with her.

She also wished that Lincoln would leave her alone and not make an appearance, because from the way her phone was buzzing and beeping like a furious insect, she knew that he was growing impatient...

*

He moved forwards slowly, he was getting quite close to the group of boys now judging by the sound, but also thought that he could now see their silhouettes against the dark night sky. His plastic mask meant that his sight was limited, but it enabled him to fit in with the theme of the day without anyone recognising him. The bushes and trees that he was walking through didn't make his task of stalking the group any easier either, hearing them was enough though, he didn't really need to be able to see them.

He approached a tall, thick tree and decided to stand behind it. The huge tree was big enough to cover him entirely, but he left part of himself visible out of necessity so that he could watch the group of boys who were messing around in the park. He was fairly certain they couldn't see him anyway, despite the bright colours of his costume and mask, there were still enough trees, bushes and leaves to ensure he remained practically invisible to them (unless they were looking for him, which of course they wouldn't be).

He saw one of the boys, in frustration, jump from a swing and sigh at his phone. Although it wasn't exactly a sigh, more of an angry growl. This boy seemed the largest of the group, fairly tall and very broad and muscular, his spikey hair shadowed against the night sky.

"Fuck's sake." He growled again, ramming his phone inside his pocket.

"Lincoln, buddy, chill out man." One of the other boys said, moving close to their friend and patting him on the back.

"Give me some of that." The boy called Lincoln snatched something from his friends' hand and held it up to his head, tilting it back as he did so. It seemed the boys had come to the park to drink alcohol. It also appeared that Lincoln was in charge of this social circle judging by the way there was no objection to his forceful theft of his friends' beer.

"I'm going to her house." Lincoln stated.

Lincoln meant Chloe's house; he knew that. He'd been keeping a close eye on Chloe all day, although she was completely unaware. He was going to isolate her, remove all obstacles in his path, before moving in to seize the prize at the end of his journey.

Like a game of chess. The queen: the most powerful, the most dangerous, the most coveted piece on the board. However, the queen is always protected by those around her, preventing anyone from getting close to her. But he was already closing in on her; one defender had been disposed of. Abby, a faithful friend, but a mere pawn in this game.

Now, Lincoln was planning on going to the queen, something that had to be stopped.

"Maybe that isn't the best idea." One of Lincoln's friends voiced his concern, although the tone of his voice demonstrated that he knew there was no argument or discussion to be had, Lincoln would be going to Chloe's house.

"I say go for it." Another friend said encouragingly, "Maybe it's the best way to finally get her to listen to you properly."

He saw Lincoln nodding, "Exactly. There's no way she'll be able to resist me when we're alone together."

He wanted a better look at Lincoln to judge that for himself, at the moment he couldn't see the features of his face, but knew that he would be seeing them soon enough.

"You sound confident." A friend tutted; the one who had quickly voiced concern at Lincoln's plan.

"Of course I'm confident. The girl loved it when we spent that night together." He chuckled slightly, "Couldn't get enough of me could she? You should have heard her."

"Funny how she hasn't come back for more. In fact, I seem to remember her rejecting you a few times, and most of them have been in front of us." The friend hit back, but laughed too, showing this was just usual competition within the pack.

Lincoln, however, was eager as ever to assert his dominance as pack leader: "Maybe I'll just take what I want, then. She'll love it either way." He walked close to his friend.

"You're twisted, man." But the friend didn't sound concerned, the words were spoken as though through grinning teeth, and his next words confirmed the lack of concern. "We could film it…"

"Now who's twisted?" Lincoln said, before quickly adding, "And no. She's all mine."

Lincoln's head tilted back again as he drank from a bottle, and then there was a crashing sound as he threw it on the floor with frustrated and fierce force, making it shatter almost thunderously in the calm of the night.

"Right, we heading to this party or what?" Lincoln asked, although it was clearly a demand more than a question; nobody would defy their mighty leader, surely? Lincoln certainly lived up to his name.

"I thought you were going to Chloe's?" One of his friends checked.

"I'll come to the party for an hour, I suppose."

It seemed that even the mighty Lincoln needed some courage before he visited the queen.

"Let's go!" One of the boys said enthusiastically.

"I need a piss first, man." That sounded like a new voice… but no, it was Lincoln, wasn't it? The voices were becoming so muddled.

"Can't it wait until we get there?" One of the friends.

"I'm desperate. I'll go in the bushes and catch up with you in a minute." Yes, it had to be Lincoln. This was the perfect opportunity.

He heard the rest of the boys start to walk away from the park whilst Lincoln approached the bushes, the sound of his zip being undone quite loud against the calmness of that cold, dark Halloween night.

He moved forward, walking slowly, trying to make sure that he didn't tread too hard on any leaves or twigs and alert his target to his presence. He couldn't walk directly in front of him, otherwise he would surely be spotted, but instead walked a little to the right of the black silhouette to ensure he was out of his targets' sight.

When he was within reaching distance, the sound that resembled running water stopped and the boy's breath caught in his throat, "Hello?"

Before Lincoln could call out for his friends, he grabbed him by the throat swiftly and firmly, beginning to crush to make sure that no sound would escape the boy's throat other than weak gasps for air. Pulling the figure towards him slightly, he raised his other hand, the hand in which he held his knife. He took great care to make sure his aim was precise, and then he slashed the cold blade across the boy's throat. He felt the warm liquid begin to spill across his hand and between his fingers. He took some delight in knowing what it was, but knew he would be washing it off as quickly as he could afterwards, preferring the ice-cold touch of the Halloween air. He waited until the choking sound and the struggling had stopped, and then released his grip, letting the heavy body fall to the floor.

He bent over, finding a patch of grass and wiping his hand on it. He knew it wouldn't get rid of all the blood, but it would at least make the remaining stains able to blend in with the fake costume blood that most people would be wearing that night.

He stepped over his victim and took hold of the head, moving to the side and hoisting the head up to the sky, trying to allow the moonlight to illuminate the face for him. It worked, but it wasn't the features of the face that he noticed first. It was the hair. The hair was flat, not spikey. This wasn't Lincoln. He had killed the wrong person.

He had felt that the voice of the person had been different, but it had sounded so similar to Lincoln. Most of the boys had sounded quite similar, and he guessed he had only been able to determine who was who by *what* they were saying, rather than *how* they were saying it. It also appeared that the mask *did* serve to partially obstruct his hearing as well as his eyesight.

He tossed the head back to the floor and stepped out of the trees, into the park. There were more people on the street now than there had been earlier, but he didn't worry about his appearance or the blood that would surely be dripping from his knife. Who would know it was the real thing?

He scanned the street, trying to locate Lincoln and his group of followers, but it seemed they had already gone.

No matter, he thought.

If he couldn't kill Lincoln now, he would kill him later.

They would both be paying Chloe a visit on that Halloween night, with the most sinister of tricks prepared for her, the treats all for him…

Chapter Eight

Jackson switched on the car's headlights, only just noticing how dark the night had become as he turned onto a narrow road with street lamps casting long yellow pools of light across the streets and houses. The city centre and surrounding areas had been alive with movement; mostly trick or treaters, school children travelling in small groups carrying their collected treats around with them, but also older students who were most likely heading to parties.

Detective Inspector Jackson slowed the car right down so that it began to creep along the road. He knew that Chloe's house was somewhere close to here – maybe on this road, or maybe down another one that connected to it. He stopped the car next to some houses, deciding that he should probably check where to go from here using the online map on his phone.

However, as he took his phone out and began to type in Chloe's address in the search bar which rested above a map of the county of Southumberland, he began to feel that going straight to Chloe's house probably wasn't the best course of action to take. He was beginning to feel that he would get there and find that there was no trouble at all, and he would scare her all for nothing. There was a very high chance that Cox the clown had simply fled, moving onto another area of the country to continue his unfinished terror. But, as Jackson had already considered that night, it was also likely that he had returned to ensure the 'lone survivor' of his horrors survived no more.

With that thought, Jackson started the car again and followed the route that his phone told him to. Eventually, after what was probably only a few seconds, he stopped his car again. Looking out of the window, he saw Chloe's house. The light in the living room was on, and so he leaned his head forward – almost head-butting the window – to try and see inside more clearly. He retreated back into the shadows of the car when a figure entered the room.

It was Chloe. He could tell just by her hair. How long had it been since he'd last seen her? Many months, almost a year. She was okay, undisturbed, he could see that now. He had overreacted earlier. However... He was here now, so why not just knock on the door? See her, talk to her, be introduced to her child...

Had she even kept it? Jackson knew that Chloe's plan had been to go to university. Did that mean she had given her child up to someone who could give it more of their time, or had she kept it and started raising it with the help of her parents as he assumed she would have?

What had she named it, if she had kept it? If it was a boy, she would have surely named him Connor, after his Father.

Chloe disappeared from view, either leaving the room or sitting down. Jackson didn't intend to stick around, but he wasn't going to leave entirely either. Chloe was safe, yes, but she also appeared to be by herself. It was entirely possible that Cox the clown was present and just waiting for the right moment to strike.

Jackson, as he would have been doing this time a year ago, intended to search the area for the killer.

Once again, he started his car and drove away, trying not to glance back at the front of Chloe's house as he did so. He had to stay close to her, close enough so that he could rush back to her house if he needed to, but also at a decent enough distance so that he could effectively search the rest of the surrounding area too.

Jackson guessed that officers would have already called Ralph Cox, maybe even been to his house to ask if he'd heard from his son and search the rooms there to make sure he wasn't protecting his son a second time.

But Jackson had to be sure. He picked up his phone and called Andy, putting the call on loudspeaker and then putting the phone on the passenger's seat.

Ring, ring.

Ring, ring.

Click.

"JJ, have you-"

"Has Ralph Cox's house been searched?"

"We sent some officers this morning but-"

"Then send some again! Search the fucking place from top to bottom! I want him questioned, I want him brought into the station. We can't take chances, Andy. If he's protecting his son again then we need to cut off that protection, then he'll eventually have to reveal himself."

"Yes, boss. But…"

"But what?"

"You know as well as I do what's become of Ralph Cox."

Jackson did know. The former Deputy Chief Constable had become a recluse for many months after last year's Halloween. Then, some months ago there had been people – officers – who had seen him roaming the streets of Tornwich. Drunk and dishevelled, looking as though he was homeless and without anywhere to go.

But Jackson didn't want to take chances.

"Call me with any updates." He commanded, and then pressed the red circle to end the call.

He parked the car a couple of hundred metres away from Chloe's house. He left the car, making sure that he had all the 'tools' he needed on his harness (he always kept his harness with him; in the back of his car or in his office, in case of nights like tonight when he thought he would need it, despite detectives not usually wearing them – continuing his tradition of breaking the norm even now, after his promotion) before leaving the car and locking it. He wouldn't knock on any doors; he didn't want to scare anyone or risk word getting back to Chloe that he was in the area searching for the person who had killed her boyfriend – the Father to her baby – and other friends because he had escaped and she was no longer safe.

No, he would simply look inside windows, in gardens and in any public areas such as parks. If there were any parties that he noticed maybe he would be able to check on those hands-on, using the excuse of just reminding everyone there to 'keep it down', while actually trying to scope out Cox the clown.

Should he have called in Andy, or any other reinforcements? No, not yet. If he discovered anything of interest he would call them, but otherwise until they got in touch with him he would leave them to sit around, talking and waiting for something to be reported that could be a link to Cox's whereabouts.

Jackson didn't even know how Cox the clown had escaped, but by the sounds of it neither did the hospital staff. *His room was unlocked and he was just… gone.* That's what Andy had said. They were clueless. Cox the clown had simply disappeared.

Maybe his Father *was* protecting him – he'd helped him escape and then kept him hidden in his house. But why would he do that? Jackson had seen the look that they had given one another on *that night* as they were both arrested. Unless Cox had snapped again and wanted to be the one to finish his son off as revenge for losing his job…

Or, and Jackson thought this was the likelier option given the reported state of Ralph Cox, Cox's clown companion had been waiting for a full year to help him escape on Halloween so that they could once again wreak havoc and create fear across an entire city.

Jackson would stay here until morning if he had to, until he was sure that Chloe would be safe from Cox the clown. Then, he would speak to Andy, get the latest before going to Ralph Cox's to see for himself that he hadn't helped – or killed – his son. If all those options led nowhere, then Jackson would finally assume that Cox the clown had simply fled, leaving Southumberland to pursue a new life elsewhere.

It was going to be a long night.

Jackson didn't care, though, he was prepared for this. He felt as though he'd been preparing for this ever since *that night* a year ago. The way he would become consumed with fear every time someone approached his office… It was as though he knew something like this was going to happen; with Ralph Cox walking free and his son's sinister sidekick still on the loose, how could he not? Every night was long, these days; Jackson constantly struggled to sleep.

A year ago he hadn't been sleeping properly because of the murders, and he had never recovered since then. He couldn't remember the last night when he'd had several hours of peaceful, uninterrupted sleep. Actually, he couldn't remember the last night he'd had when nightmares hadn't haunted his sleep.

Giant bunnies wielding axes. Dismembered, decapitated teenagers lying beneath the towering trees of the forest. Clowns running through the trees, laughing and slashing maniacally.

His sister… Her still body, her lifeless eyes watching him…

Bodies in Wald Forest…

They had returned.

*

Lincoln put the cold bottle to his lips and tilted his head back, trying to drink its contents as quickly as he could. His friend had just handed him a new bottle, but he wanted to leave the party now. He had already been there for nearly an hour, he had to go to Chloe's now. *Had to.*

Drinking the beer wasn't even enjoyable or pleasant anymore. He just needed to get it over with so that he could leave. He waited until the friend who had handed him the bottle had moved away and was slurring his words at other people and falling on them occasionally, and then he set the bottle down on the nearest table before heading towards the front door. Everyone was already too drunk to care that he had left without saying goodbye, so he just walked through the crowds of people while trying not to make eye contact until he reached the front door.

Thankfully, nobody tried to talk to him or got in his way too much.

When he was out on the street the quietness and coldness of the Halloween night attacked him swiftly. His ears struggled to adjust from the loud environment he had just exited and he felt deaf for a few moments, apart from the endless ringing sound. The warmth of the house, generated by the masses of people and their energy, was slashed away by the ice-cold air of the dark night.

He fumbled around with the zip of his jacket as he left the house's front garden, his fingers already shaking violently as they struggled against the bitter coldness. Eventually, some seconds later, he managed to get a grip on the zip and pull it all the way up to his neck.

He shoved his hands inside his coat pockets and let his eyes wander across the streets surrounding him. There were groups upon groups of trick or treaters now, mostly small children in groups of what he guessed were friends and siblings, but many groups were also accompanied by parents.

He distracted himself from the groups of zombies, vampires, witches and ghosts by thinking about his arrival at Chloe's. He'd knock on the door. He wasn't going to just invite himself in, although that would show confidence... No. He couldn't do that. It would scare her too much. A display of confidence or not, he didn't want her getting scared straight away. He had to try and be calm at first, try one more time to talk her round. If he couldn't...

Maybe then would be the time to scare her.

He wanted her. Even if it was just one more time, he *wanted* her.

She wanted him, too. He knew it. He could *feel* it. Every time they were close to one another, every time he would talk to her and ask her out, he could feel the desire within her. He saw the way she looked at him – the way she *still* looked at him, the way she had done that first night in the nightclub. Then they had spent that amazing night together…

He was aware of her position, he knew who she was, but why should that change anything? Just because she had a baby and had been through some tough times didn't mean he should give her any special treatment, surely? She'd never mentioned it, and she seemed to be fine every time he spoke to her or was with her. What she had been through clearly hadn't left that much of a scar. Mental of physical.

But he wanted to know more. He still had a strong interest in serial killers, and had closely followed the events of last year's Halloween. He had been so close to the action without knowing it, and he even remembered seeing Chloe and her boyfriend that night when everyone was gathered around the bonfire.

Now, he had experienced her for himself, but he wanted more. He had a chance to talk to someone who'd survived the terror of being held captive by a serial killer, how could he let the opportunity slip away? Perhaps he should have brought it up sooner, on that night they had spent together… but that would have been a bit of a mood killer, surely.

Chloe hadn't been the girl he'd assumed she was. He thought the character he'd made himself into worked – and it did, just not on girls like Chloe. He'd thought she was a popular girl after seeing her for the first time on that Halloween night, and after seeing her boyfriend. But she wasn't. She was… normal.

The night they had spent together had been special to him. He felt as though he'd been able to actually be himself for the first time in a very long while. But now he was caught in a trap; he had been wearing the mask for so long that it had become stuck to his face. He couldn't remove it… was it possible that the character he had moulded for himself was actually the person he was becoming?

Lincoln looked up to see where he was. He was still a few minutes away from Chloe's. He looked around and saw that there were still plenty of groups of trick or treaters around, but there were much fewer in this part of the city, away from the centre where most people would be gathered or heading towards. It was relatively quiet in this area. Thankfully.

Lincoln kept his gaze ahead as he walked down the street, and saw someone not too far ahead of him who looked just as out of place as he did – they were not wearing a Halloween costume. He examined the person as he got closer to them, and saw that they were wearing a harness over their shirt with many different items hanging from it. With the distance and darkness between them, Lincoln couldn't make them out, but as he picked up his pace he saw the handcuffs shine in the moonlight. It looked like he was going to have to keep his visit to Chloe's as civil as possible… or maybe just as quiet as possible.

Lincoln finally reached the bald man with the handcuffs on his harness. Then, the harness and the equipment on it disappeared from view as the man covered his top half with a jacket. He put it on casually, seemingly not afraid of anyone seeing the items he was carrying with him. He thought the man had been wearing ordinary clothes, but hadn't been able to tell from the distance before, but as he walked alongside him he could see that he was wearing 'normal' clothes. There was no police uniform. So this wasn't a regular policeman patrolling the area… something different.

"Happy Halloween." Lincoln said, slowing his pace to walk side by side with the man. He could see the big, black, bushy beard now as the man turned to face him for the first time.

The man nodded, "You too." Lincoln thought that was all the man was going to say, but then he showed interest in making some small talk, or maybe gathering information on whatever he was in the area for. "Going to a party?" He asked casually – or maybe he was only trying to sound casual.

"Just left one." Lincoln answered, "Going to my girlfriend's now."

"Oh, Halloween date night?"

"Sort of." Lincoln nodded, and then tried to be casual just as the policeman had been, "You keeping an eye out for trouble? Won't find much in this part of the city."

The man turned and looked at Lincoln again, an eyebrow cocked as though questioning how he knew he was a policeman.

"If you don't want people to know your job," Lincoln began, "You really should keep that harness thing covered up."

"Oh." The man replied, and then opened his jacket, pulling it around to his back, looked down at his harness, but didn't pull his coat back over it for some time. "No. I'm not trying to be stealthy."

Lincoln noted how the man was being very vague and had completely avoided his earlier question.

"Well," The policeman sighed, "I've walked up and down this road enough times now. Hope you and your girlfriend have a good night." He stopped walking and turned, leaning on a street lamp and looking across the road.

Lincoln followed his gaze. Another street lamp. Nothing of interest. Nothing at all, really.

Lincoln didn't say anything else and just turned, carrying on his journey. That hadn't been as informative or entertaining as he thought it would be. The policeman was either very bored, or on a very important job that meant he couldn't be disturbed.

Never mind, Lincoln thought, he was nearly at Chloe's now. Just a few houses away…

*

Chloe heard her phone ringing, and almost instantly felt blood rushing to her chest. It turned warm; like a fire of panic had rushed through her body. She brought her hands up to her head and rubbed her eyelids, sighing as she did so.

Please don't be him.

She rose from the bed and slowly started to walk out of the room, hoping she could make the phone ring and ring until it stopped. She would have to speak to Lincoln eventually, she knew that, but she wanted to avoid him for as long as she could. She worried about the noise waking Jackson up, but thought – hoped – that the noise wouldn't carry upstairs.

Where is Abby?

Chloe took the stairs one at a time. Her breathing had become unsteady and she could feel her hand shaking as she held lightly onto the bannister. This wasn't normal… She always felt uncomfortable around Lincoln, but never this bad. This was *fear*.

Boys being obsessed with her on Halloween night dug up some bad memories, she supposed.

She reached her phone and approached it slowly, and saw that the name flashing on the screen wasn't Lincoln, but her Auntie E. She quickly snatched the phone up from the sofa and answered it.

"Auntie E! Sorry, I was just upstairs with Jackson, everything okay?"

"Yes, sweetheart, everything is fine. How are you?"

"I'm good thank you."

"Oh, good." She heard her Aunt sigh. Relief? Was she phoning to check up on her because it was Halloween? "Your Mother called." There was her answer.

"Oh?" Chloe voiced, asking her Auntie to elaborate.

"She said you had a friend coming over and that her and your Father had gone out. I was wondering if you wanted me to come and pick Jackson up for you? I know how needed a girls' night in can be sometimes." Her Auntie chuckled, and Chloe rolled her eyes but found herself smiling at the same time.

"Thanks, Auntie E, but I'm honestly fine. It's just going to be me and Abby and it's not like we're getting drunk."

"Well, I'm coming to get him anyway." She stated happily, "Seb is away tonight at work so I'm a bit bored to be honest with you. It's been a few weeks since you've had a night without him, anyway, hasn't it? I'm coming to get him, he can spend the night with me."

"Looking after him isn't a job to me, you know, Auntie E? Everyone makes it sound that way."

"Oh! No, I don't mean it to sound that way, my love! It's just good to have a break sometimes, and it lets the rest of us see him. Is it okay if I pick him up? I could just use the company, really."

Chloe knew that this was her parents' doing, and as much as she loved having Jackson with her, she knew that her Auntie – and her parents – were right. Chloe checked the clock on the wall and saw that it wasn't too late for Jackson's sleep to be disturbed. It was Halloween, anyway, today could be a treat for him in terms of bedtimes and other such rules. She'd already let him have too many naps for far too long today, anyway. "If you wouldn't mind then, Auntie E."

"Of course not! I'll be there shortly." She said, and then Chloe heard the beep as her Auntie hung up.

Chloe pulled the phone away from her ear and looked out the living room window. No sign of Abby. No sign of Lincoln.

She held up her phone again and sent a text to Abby asking what time she was planning on coming over.

Then, she went back up the stairs to start preparing Jackson for a night at Auntie E's.

*

She took the phone away from her ear and put it in her pocket. Her sister had phoned her only a few minutes ago requesting that she talk to Chloe and have Jackson sleep at hers for the night. She didn't mind, she was more than happy to, especially considering what day it was. Chloe deserved to be with her friends and relax, taking her mind off all the bad memories that must now come with Halloween.

She tried to stand up but felt herself fall back down into her seat. She thought she had slipped for a moment, but then felt something pressing on the top of her head, holding her down so firmly that her neck started to hurt. The pain starting to feel as though her neck was about to collapse into her body.

Just as she was about to scream, something glimmered in front of her face, forcing the sound to become trapped in her throat. The knife was held by a hand, a hand stained by a dried, dark red. The arm was covered in a thin, loose material. Orange. Bright orange. Whoever was behind her, holding her still in her seat, had brought the knife in front of her to make her silent. She tried to speak, to ask who it was, to ask what they wanted, but no words came.

She closed her eyes, pressed her eyelids so tightly together the tears could no longer drip down her cheeks.

She felt the cold steel press against her throat.

She held her breath.

Then, she never breathed again.

Chapter Nine

Lincoln began to walk more slowly, he could see her house now, and he wanted to calm his breathing and slow his heart rate before knocking on the door. He had to appear calm and confident, not nervous, and he couldn't scare her – not until he was through the door, at least. He took in deep breaths, and felt himself begin to calm down, his pulse slowed and his hands stopped shaking. He'd never been this nervous before, but this was her house, it was more personal. Not only that, but it was more private. They would be alone. If he could get inside the house, anyway, which he was determined to do.

Her parents were out, just as he'd hoped. If they had been in, he might not have been able to follow through with his plan properly... Maybe he would have asked her to walk with him, or maybe he could have got her to invite him up to her room so they could talk privately. There were no cars outside the front of the house, and already he could see Chloe's silhouette against the living room window. It wasn't there for very long; she must have walked into another room.

Lincoln walked across the front garden and turned as he reached the path leading up to the front door. He slowly took each step towards the door, remembering Chloe's features as he did so. When he thought of her, he liked to think of that night they had spent together. The way her blonde hair had been free and loose, waving around as their bodies were pressed together, tossing and turning as they moved as one, locked in passion. The way her eyes were brighter and wider than ever, the way they examined him with such attraction. Her mouth as it parted slightly just before it moved towards his, and then the lips as they wrapped themselves around his own...

He barely realised he'd knocked the front door until it was pulled open. The light pouring out of the house, illuminating the beautiful lady that stood before him. Her features were there, the same ones that he could remember from that night. Except the hair was tied back neatly now, the eyes were wide with shock rather than pleasure, and the lips parted slightly, but twisted with distaste rather than by a desire to kiss.

For a moment he feared she would slam the door in his face, but her muscles relaxed. The grip of her hand on the door loosened, her eyelids came closer together and her lips did the same. However, she still didn't say anything or step aside to allow Lincoln inside, so he thought he better start explaining himself quickly if he was going to achieve what he had come here to do and gain entry...

*

Chloe stood and stared at Lincoln. She was mentally screaming at herself, believing she should have check who was at the door from the living room window before actually opening it, but she had thought it was Auntie E come to pick up Jackson. She hadn't even thought it would be anyone else – even Abby didn't cross her mind after the knock at the door.

She wanted to shut the door and lock him out, but feared that would just make him more determined, as that was the effect rejection always seemed to have on him. Also, there appeared to be something different about him this time... He was alone, and the 'cool boy' smile that seemed to be permanently plastered across his face was gone, along with the body language that came with it. Was he being himself? The boy she'd met in the club that night? Or had he simply brought the act back as a last resort to win her back?

"Chloe…" He stepped forward slightly, and as much as she wanted to shut the door and block him out, it all felt different; even the way he had said her name. He didn't sound like the 'cool boy' he had been for the past few weeks, but more like the nice guy she had met a couple of months ago during the first week of university.

Almost in a trance, as though he was controlling her mind, she stepped backwards and gave him space to enter the house. He didn't come in straight away, but looked at her as though in shock. He considered the space she had left for him to come in, still looking bewildered, as though he expected to have the door slammed in his face. She had wanted to do that, of course, because of the way Lincoln had been over the past few weeks. But he wasn't acting like that now, so she guessed curiosity had got the better of her and she had stepped aside to let him in.

Part of her hated him and wanted him out of the house; the way he had been recently made her feel as though he didn't deserve any of her time.

Part of her hoped the real Lincoln was the one she had met in the club and he had come here to show her that.

One of these had to be the act, but which one? Had Lincoln moulded a character for himself in order to fit in with his friends, or had he created an alter ego for when he wanted to attract girls?

She watched him walk inside the living room and followed after him. They stood, staring at one another for a few moments before she gestured for him to sit.

"I thought you had Jackson?" He asked.

"He's asleep in my room."

"Still?"

"Babies nap a lot, Lincoln."

"Oh." He pushed his bottom lip out and nodded, as though he had just been told an interesting fact.

Chloe sat next to him on the sofa, but was careful to ensure there was distance between them, "What are you doing here?"

"I just wanted to see you." He said, and looked at her, his brown eyes wide like a teddy bear's.

"Lincoln…" She sighed and looked away, but he edged slightly closer to her and so she returned her gaze to him.

"If you didn't want to see me you wouldn't have let me in the house." He stated, and Chloe didn't respond, how could she deny it? She *did* want to see him, but in the hope that this was the Lincoln she had spent a night with in his university flat, not the one who had been almost stalking her afterwards.

His hand reached out towards her leg, and brushed against it lightly before she clasped her own hand over his, "Lincoln." She said firmly.

"What?" He smirked, the 'cool boy' returning.

Shit! She screamed at herself; how could she have been so stupid?

"You know you want me." He breathed, and leaned forward as though he wanted to kiss her, but not fully closing his eyes so he could watch her as he leaned in and judge her response.

She stood from the sofa, and watched as he almost fell face-first onto a cushion. She would have laughed if she wasn't beginning to get so worried. She was in the house alone with him (apart from Jackson, but there wasn't much he could do if the situation was to turn heated), and began to fear that her rejection would only spur Lincoln on as it had been doing recently.

"Get the fuck out!" She demanded, and flung an arm in the direction of the front door. She hated him, but she hated herself, too. Why had she let him in the house? Was she really more lonely and desperate than she realised? Worse than that, why had she slept with him in the first place? A boy she barely knew and had only just met. All the rational reasons she usually listed in her mind were gone now; she wasn't a young student who 'should be enjoying herself', she was a Mother who had to think about the future. She shouldn't have let her family talk her into believing the former.

She wanted Connor. As Lincoln rose from the sofa, she had to fight back tears at the thought of his loving blue eyes, the way they seemed to smile at her all by themselves…

Lincoln unzipped his coat and threw it to the floor, revealing his broad chest and thick, toned arms. There was no way she was getting past him and there was no way she could reason with him. She felt trapped. He came closer and closer towards her, in a memory all too sinisterly similar to what had happened last year.

The clown as he unzipped the tent and stepped inside, watching her for a few moments before he had started coming towards her. She had been trapped then, as well. There was no way of getting past him and out of the tent, no way of reasoning with a psychopathic killer to let her free… But she had done something else. Something that had brought her some time before being saved. Abby was meant to be coming. Her Auntie, as well, to pick Jackson up. Her parents should be home soon. She had to give herself that extra time… As he came closer and closer towards her, she had said…

"I'm pregnant!" She shouted it this time, not being able to speak the words calmly in her panicked state.

He stopped and stared at her. His reaction the same as the madman's had been a year ago; the look of shock quickly replacing the one of delight.

He looked her up and down for a few moments, was her lie that obvious? She would have had to have been pregnant for about a month now, and she guessed Lincoln was doing some quick maths in his head, too. The clown hadn't been this disbelieving, it had taken no convincing at all, but then it was a bad lie; even Lincoln wasn't stupid enough to see through it.

His smile returned, "And it's taken you this long to tell me?"

Chloe held a hand up to her eyes and sucked in a shaky breath, "Please just go, Lincoln."

But then she felt his hands quickly seize her. They squeezed tightly before forcing her to the floor. She saw Lincoln drop on top of her next, grabbing her arms and pinning them above her head. He started to kiss her neck. She tried to kick out, but he was too heavy for her legs to have any great effect.

His head almost collided with hers as he smashed his lips forcefully against hers. She felt her arms pressed together and held by one hand instead of two. His other hand… she could feel it, working its way down her body. Then, it left hers and went to his, and she heard a zip being undone.

She whimpered and thought of Connor again. The clown had done this to him. This is how he must have felt... So scared, and trapped, and alone...

*

Jackson looked across the street and saw a park surrounded by bushes and large trees; a small woodland area that stretched down a long road, across the back of many houses. He had already seen it earlier that night, when he had been walking the opposite direction, but now he was walking back down the road and to his car. He had given up. There was nothing. Chloe was safe.

He had wanted to phone Andy to see where he was and what the situation at the psychiatric hospital was, but when searching his pockets for his phone, he discovered it wasn't there. He must have left it in the car. He had thought it strange that nobody had contacted him over the last few hours, but now realised that they might have been trying to. Maybe something *had* happened. Maybe Cox the clown had already been caught and Jackson had unnecessarily been searching Chloe's neighbourhood for the past few hours.

Jackson crossed the road and walked alongside the park. He slowed his pace and examined the bushes surrounding it. He looked across all of them, looking for even the smallest leaf out of place as a sign of someone being there. Still, there was nothing. Nothing in the bushes, at least. Jackson looked at the concrete floor and saw the dark red liquid that had been spilled across it. Not just a small amount, but a large, thick pool. It was bordering with the small woodland, in the corner of the park, spilling out from a small bush. How had he missed that before?

Jackson quickly sped towards the pool of blood, looking around the make sure no curious trick or treaters had followed him or seen the liquid too. Was it real blood? Or was it part of a Halloween trick someone was playing?

He reached the dark red pool and followed it into the bushes, across the leaves and to the woodland ground, where a pair of stunned, lifeless eyes stared up at the night sky.

Jackson recoiled. He let his eyes, just for a moment, look at the gaping wound of the slashed throat. Then, he turned around and started running. He had to get to his car, he had to contact Andy. Cox the clown was here, after all, returning to cause Halloween horror once again.

*

It had taken Andy almost an hour to drive from the psychiatric hospital, into Tornwich city centre and then the surrounding neighbourhoods to try and locate Jackson's car. Thankfully, Andy had a vague recollection of where the girl who had survived last year's massacre lived.

He slowed his car down and parked it behind Jackson's.

He had been trying to contact Jackson for hours. Phoning him with no breakthrough. He guessed that Jackson, in his rush, must have left it in his car. Had he really been searching all this time? Andy almost didn't want to tell Jackson the news he had come to tell him, because it was sure to make him feel very foolish and as though he had wasted his time.

Andy got out of his car and walked towards Jackson's. He pressed his face up against the driver's window and looked inside. As he'd suspected, Jackson's phone was in the car, on the passenger's seat.

Andy took a step back and looked around, "JJ?" He whispered into the calmness of the night, "JJ, are you here?"

When he got no response he looked down again at the car. He saw his own reflection in the window, and then a white circle beside it which he had assumed was the moon. But it couldn't be the moon, he had just seen the moon, and it was above the houses on the other side of the street.

Andy held his breath as he turned his head to see a plastic clown mask. He began to ready himself for a struggle but it was too late, he was grabbed by the throat and pulled off his feet with one arm. The other, orange-sleeved arm held a knife high in the air, and then brought it forward again and again and again, each impact of the large, shiny and sharp weapon thudding loudly into Andy, the noise echoing through the calm Halloween night.

Andy, in his last sequence of thoughts, wondered how it was all possible, and wondered just who was beneath that frowning clown mask…

Chapter Ten

Jackson was struggling to breathe, but his car was now in sight. He slowed down to a fast walk and tried to catch his breath as much as he could. As he approached the car, he saw a body lying next to it, eyes wide and staring into the blackness of the night just as the last one's had been. Except Jackson knew these eyes, he knew this face; Andy.

He crouched down, heart hammering against his chest, sweat dripping from his body. He reached down to touch Andy, but then saw the several red holes across his abdomen, leaking wet fluid across his shirt. Instead, he rested his fingers lightly on Andy's head.

"Shit." He whispered, and then closed his eyes.

He didn't have time to mourn right now.

He stood and unlocked his car, reached across the driver's seat and grabbed his phone. The moment he unlocked it, it started to ring. A number that was unknown to him flashed up on the screen, but he answered it anyway and held the phone to his ear, hoping that help would be on the other end.

"Hello?"

"Detective Inspector Jackson?"

"Yes?"

"This is Dr Lunn from the psychiatric hospital, has Sergeant Andrew been in touch with you yet?"

Jackson paused, looked down at Andy's dead body, and then responded: "Andy's here…"

"Oh, good, then he's told you-"

"He's dead."

There was a long, uncomfortable silence, and Jackson could hear Dr Lunn's breathing become faster and heavier on the other end of the line.

"Detective…" Dr Lunn said, but didn't finish whatever he wanted to say, and Jackson was tired of people hiding things from him today.

"Tell me what you need to." He ordered.

"Cox… 'the clown'… as your men refer to him. He's dead."

Jackson closed his eyes and tried to make sense of what he'd just been told, but so many things were piling up in his mind that he couldn't. "What?" He just about whispered.

"We found him in the forest at the back of the hospital. It looks as though he hung himself – from a tree – but… Well…" There was a chance Cox the clown had been killed, not committed suicide; Jackson knew that's what Dr Lunn was telling him.

"Dr Lunn. Andy has been killed. I found another body some minutes ago. There is someone here killing people, and you're telling me Cox is dead?"

"Detective…" Dr Lunn paused, but only for a moment, perhaps remembering Jackson's impatience. His words not only ended the silence, but cut through it like a blade, and what he said sent Jackson's mind, breath and heart racing in fear and confusion: "I don't know who is there… *killing people*… but whoever it is… *it's not Cox the clown.*"

*

Chloe tried to pull her hands free from Lincoln's grip, but she couldn't. She tried thrusting her body upwards to throw him off, or at least cause enough instability to make him unbalanced and distracted so she could wriggle free, but he was too heavy and made remarks mocking her attempts ("See? I knew you wanted it!" being the most repeated line).

Although she couldn't get free, she was determined to make this as difficult as possible for him. He had unzipped his own trousers, but was having a hard time doing the same to hers. Her thrusting meant that he couldn't get a decent grip on the zip, and when he did get a slight grip his hand just kept slipping from it.

"Fuck's sake! Keep still!" He shouted, and she couldn't help but laugh. He was so frustrated and angry, unable to do what he wanted, and she knew that eventually this struggle alone would tire them out. It was just a matter of whether she could outlast Lincoln. Probably not, considering his physical state, but she was going to try her best.

As she laughed at him, he stopped for a moment and stared at her. His eyes were angry, but his raised eyebrows showed his shock. She quickly regretted her mocking and insulting action, because instead of fumbling with her zip, he simply gripped the top of her trousers and started pulling. Then she started to panic again.

*

Jackson threw his phone back in the car and shut the door. He reached for his harness, took out his baton and flicked it outwards, the end shooting out. He looked around for a moment, trying to remember which way to go in order to get to Chloe's house. He was in a daze; everything seemed blurred and he struggled to remember where he had to go.

Calm down, he told himself, *think back, and trace your steps.* He remembered that afternoon and parking outside Chloe's house. He'd driven away from the house after that for fear of bumping into her and having to explain why he was there. He hadn't travelled far away from her house, though, just around the corner...

He looked to the left and remembered. He walked around Andy's body, and mentally apologised to him, but thought that his friend would understand.

If the killer wasn't Cox the clown, there was only one other person it could be.

It had to be his little helper; his 'sidekick', the short, fat clown.

It had to be.

Jackson started running again, he had to get to Chloe's house quickly if he was going to make sure that no harm came to her, and potentially her baby...

*

Chloe saw that her thrusting was doing her no favours as Lincoln tugged on her trousers. Instead of hindering his progress, it was helping him; allowing her trousers to fall further and further down her legs. She stopped and looked at how far he'd gotten them, and was surprised (but happy) to see that he hadn't gotten them as far down as she thought he had.

She thought quickly, and settled on a new tactic. She started to wriggle downwards, and it began to counteract Lincoln's tugging, the trousers staying where they were rather than going any further down or up.

She heard him grunt in frustration again, and in an apparent lapse of concentration, he brought his other arm down to start tugging on her trousers. Her arms were now free, she couldn't believe it! How had he been so stupid? She didn't dwell on it too much; but rather decided to act quickly.

However, as she was raising her fists to bring them crashing down on Lincoln's head, he fell backwards. She didn't spend any time wondering how or why, instead pulling her trousers up and jumping to her feet, ready to run as fast as she could from the house.

It was then that she saw that Lincoln hadn't fallen – he'd been pulled off her.

Now Lincoln was lying on *his* back, staring scared at something.

She followed his gaze to the figure standing in her living room, dressed in an all-in-one Halloween costume; one side jet black and the other bright orange. The figure's entire head was covered in a thick, white clown mask. The head turned slowly to look at her. The nose was a small red ball, the bright blue lips were turned downwards in a miserable grimace. The holes cut out for the eyes were black-rimmed. She looked into the holes and at the eyes that were staring at her intently.

Eyes that she knew.

She took a step backwards, but the clown turned his attention back to Lincoln, who was trying to get to his feet. She saw this out the corner of her eye; all the time keeping her gaze fixed on the clown who was standing completely motionless, its head cocked slightly to one side, inquisitively watching Lincoln trying to scrabble to his feet with his trousers around his ankles. She examined him, and saw the splashes of red across his costume. She hoped it was just fake Halloween blood, but she knew deep down that it wasn't.

The clown suddenly burst into action, raising a huge fist, and in an orange-black flash, punched Lincoln with a sickening blow.

She looked at Lincoln, and saw him fall backwards. Blood was pouring down one side of his face. It was then she realised that the clown hadn't punched Lincoln at all, he'd slashed a knife across his face. The clown, like a bull who had seen the redness of the blood, charged forward and tackled Lincoln against the wall. It held him there, let him struggle helplessly for a few moments as though enjoying his desperation. Then, the clown, in short, sharp jabs, started driving his knife into Lincoln's belly, his side, his chest.

Chloe watched blood pour from the boy who had caused her so much grief since starting university. It splattered across the wall and dripped onto the carpet. The clown released his grip and let the limp body drop to the floor, splashing in what was already a pool of blood. Chloe almost dropped to the floor and rushed to Lincoln, but then remembered what he was about to do to her before the clown had arrived.

She looked away from the clown. She had time to run from the house and be free, but she couldn't. She had to go upstairs, she had to try and protect her baby. The front door to the house was open; she hadn't locked it when she'd let Lincoln in, and that was how the clown must have got inside the house.

Just as the clown began to turn, she ran in desperation, rushing out of the room and up the stairs.

So many times before she had been through this. Waking up in the middle of the night, going downstairs for a drink and then having to make the journey back up the stairs. In the still darkness of the night, she would always panic and sprint up the stairs, not caring if the noise woke the rest of the house up. It was always silly; there was never anyone chasing her up those stairs. But now there was, and she was well-prepared for it thanks to her overactive imagination.

She took the stairs two at a time, never daring to look back for fear of what she'd see there, and also so she didn't lose her balance and fall. If he was behind her, she couldn't hear him. But he had to be there. Maybe he was walking, taking his time to enjoy her fear, closing in on his prey like a predator playfully stalking and chasing its prey before ending its life brutally and mercilessly.

When she reached the top of the stairs, she almost forgot which way to turn in order to reach her room and almost stopped dead, making her nearly lose her balance. However, she recovered on the last step by gripping onto the banister and using it to propel her around the corner and on the path towards her bedroom.

She slammed her bedroom door shut as she entered. She saw the cot at the other end of the room, but she couldn't go to it yet. She had to barricade herself in the room while she had the chance, find any weapon she could use and then look for a way out if she had time.

Her wardrobe was up against the wall, bordering the door. It was taller than the doorway and made of thick wood. It was conveniently placed – all she had to do was push it over onto its side, and it would buy her some more time. The clown would be able to push it out of the way eventually, or smash his way through the door, she was sure of that. She just needed time.

As she moved over to the wardrobe she listened. Her breath almost caught in her throat even though she knew what she was going to hear. Footsteps. Slow. He was walking down the hallway, the floorboards underneath the carpet creaking beneath his feet. They were getting louder, which meant he was coming closer.

She grabbed the wardrobe around the sides and starting pushing it downwards. It was heavy, and as soon as it was tilted far enough she knew that she wouldn't be able to retain control of it. She wanted to make it as quiet as she could, though; there was still a chance the clown hadn't seen where she'd gone. She also didn't want to wake Jackson. She wanted him to sleep, she didn't want him to remember any of this. She wanted him to know about it when he was older, but from her.

The wardrobe was halfway across the door now, and she still had control over it, but could feel it pushing down hard on her skin, digging into her bones. She let go and there was a loud *thud!* as it crashed onto the floor. Her fingers stung and she clenched her hands into tight fists, letting out a whimper in order to hold back the cry of pain that had almost escaped her throat.

The wardrobe, even on its side, covered most of the door, and with the wood it was made out of and all the clothes and shoes it held inside of it, it would act as a good temporary barrier.

As Chloe scanned the room, a thought struck her. A thought that filled her with dread and made her tear up instantly. What if the clown had already been upstairs? What if, while she was struggling with Lincoln in the living room, the clown had already been up here, in her room?

She turned towards the cot, and a part of her didn't want to go over to it and look down, but she had to.

She sped over to it and looked down at Jackson, who was still asleep.

Thank God, she thought, and then considered how remarkable it was that the baby was still sleeping. *What if he's not asleep?* Part of her mind questioned, *what if you were right, and the clown has been up here already?* She panicked for just a moment, reached down to touch him, and he stirred. She let out a shaky sigh of relief.

Relief that lasted a mere second.

She stood and looked around the room, searching for a weapon to use against the clown when it came for her, as it undoubtedly would.

She was about to start searching the drawers of her bedside table, when there was a knocking on her bedroom door. Three short, light knocks a couple of seconds apart. Next, he would try the door, and then he would start trying to break his way through. She was sure of it. She had to act quickly. There was no way to escape now. She was going to have to fight. Maybe then, just maybe, there would be a slim chance of getting out of the house alive with Jackson.

If only she had her phone, she could phone the police, and they would surely be here before the clown was able to work his way into her room. But she'd left her phone downstairs, it was on the sofa. She'd never put it back in her pocket after Lincoln's arrival, and hadn't thought to pick it up when she ran upstairs; everything had just happened so fast.

She stood in the middle of her bedroom and looked around. What was she going to use? There was nothing. Anything that could be of any use to her would be in the kitchen or somewhere else downstairs. The best she could use against the masked maniac in her bedroom were books and pens.

Suddenly, her bedroom door was flung open, but then crashed against the back of the wardrobe she had place in front of it. An arm covered in thin, orange material appeared through the small gap, and the large hand of the killer clown gripped the door and started to shove forcefully. The wardrobe started to budge with each push, edging more and more outwards, allowing more light from the hallway to pour into the bedroom – the shadow of the masked clown spilling across her bed.

Bang! Bang! Bang!

The bedroom door kept slamming against the back of the wardrobe. He was so close to being able to get in now, the wardrobe putting up less and less resistance as it moved further outwards into the room.

She looked around frantically, almost screaming with desperation.

She was about to launch onto her bed in order to attack the clown through the gap in the door, but out of nowhere, a strong kick blasted the door open and sent the wardrobe toppling onto its front. The bedroom door was wide open now, letting the light from the hallway fully penetrate her room. The grisly silhouette of the dark figure filled the doorway, casting a long, black shadow across her bedroom.

She stood, hiding Jackson from view. She was not going to let this clown past her. She would fight and die if she had to. She would punch, kick, scratch; do anything she had to in order to defend her baby.

Back straight, chest puffed out, she prepared to kill the maniac in front of her with her bare hands.

He stepped forward, and she spread her fingers out, nails long and sharp like a cat ready to strike.

Then, he fell forwards and onto his knees.

Then, something cracked thunderously across his neck.

Then, another figure filled the doorway.

"Jackson." Chloe breathed.

*

"Chloe." Detective Inspector Jackson responded, letting his baton fall to the floor. He rushed forward, Chloe doing the same. They met in the middle of her room, and he hoisted her up in his arms and held her close, feeling her hair brush lightly against his face.

He let her down and pulled back, keeping his hands on her shoulders and peering over them. "The baby, is it okay?" He asked; he was breathing heavily, his lungs felt as though they were on fire.

Chloe nodded, "Yes, he's fine." She turned her head and looked down at the baby herself. Jackson moved forwards with her and looked down at the tiny person who, despite all the action of the last few seconds, was sleeping peacefully. "His name is Jackson." He heard Chloe say.

He looked at her and smiled, "What?"

She smiled back at him and laughed as though embarrassed, "I called him Jackson. After you. His last name is Morris – that was Connor's."

Jackson nodded, "I remember."

He felt the connection between them again.

Jackson turned and looked at the body that was still lying lifelessly in the middle of Chloe's room. He slowly stepped forward and bent over the body, forcefully grabbing hold of it and turning it over so it lay on its back. Jackson held a hand across the man's throat, searching for any sign of breathing or a pulse. Neither were there.

Jackson knew who it was now. He had known as soon as he saw the figure standing in the doorway to Chloe's bedroom. It was too tall to be Cox the clown's sidekick – much too tall – and with Cox the clown himself dead it left only one person.

Jackson gripped the bottom of the plastic mask and ripped it from the man's head, revealing the face of Ralph Cox.

Epilogue

"Third time lucky." Chloe said, and smiled at Jackson.

"Looks that way." He nodded and smiled back at her.

It was Halloween night, and they were just about to put Jackson – the baby – to bed. Chloe had never envisaged a scenario in which she would be living with two Jacksons; one her child and the other the man she loved. At first it had been annoying; the two males often becoming confused as to which one she was talking to when she spoke their name. Eventually, Jackson – the detective – had told her to call him by his nickname; 'JJ', and that was that problem resolved.

It seemed as though this Halloween night was going to remain a quiet one for them as it had been all day long (*as quiet as family gatherings can be, anyway,* Chloe smiled to herself). All of the family had almost gone now, only her Mom, Dad and one or two others remained in the house.

Chloe's fears had mostly disappeared now; with both Cox the clowns dead, there was little to fear. Of course, the original Cox the clown's sidekick still hadn't been found or heard from, and there had been no clue as to his whereabouts. Chloe lived with Jackson – JJ – now, though, and that was a big help in ensuring her fears were contained.

Last year, on Halloween night, Ralph Cox had called in yet another favour from his many connections. Despite his tarnished reputation, he'd managed to get his son released from the psychiatric hospital in the early hours of that Halloween morning. From what the police could put together, and by questioning the staff at the hospital who had helped Ralph Cox, he walked his son into Wald Forest and murdered him by hanging him from a tree, making it appear as a suicide. Then he had travelled to Chloe's neighbourhood, killed Abby, a friend of Lincoln's, her Auntie, Jackson's friend Andy, and Lincoln before finally being silenced by Jackson in her bedroom.

She walked over to the bedroom window and looked across the street.

Now it was over.

I'm free.

Then, maniacal, high-pitched laughter.

Then, a clown appeared beneath the street lamp.

Then, the lights went out; the streetlamps, the house lights, everything.

Then, nothing.

May – October, 2017

Printed in Poland
by Amazon Fulfillment
Poland Sp. z o.o., Wrocław